"Don't think," Chris urged. "Just say yes."

"I think that's how I got into trouble twelve years ago." Anne smiled at him, anyway, loving the way his voice deepened whenever he wanted his own way.

He stood up, keeping a grip on her hand. "I want to be part of Martha's life and yours. Our daughter would like that."

"You're playing dirty." Chris wasn't the man for her, Anne firmly reminded herself.

"I'll play any way I can." His fingers caressed her and he pulled her toward him. His breath feathered against her lips as he bent over her. "I've already lost twelve years." Then his lips touched hers, demanding, warm, persistent.

Her lips parted, as naturally as the feelings that swept over her. She remembered the way he tasted and the way his body felt against hers, inside hers, around hers. And realized that if the embrace continued, as his palms slid underneath her T-shirt and cupped her breasts, that she could be making love with him if she didn't stop.

She didn't want to stop, though. That was the problem.

Talented and popular **Kristine Rolofson** continues to delight her many fans with her warm and moving love stories. A resident of Rhode Island, she likes to write about this beautiful locale in her books. The joy of family is a recurring theme in Kristine's books, a theme that Kristine knows a lot about since she is the mother of six. *Baby Blues* is her tenth published novel.

Books by Kristine Rolofson

HARLEQUIN TEMPTATION

Don't miss any of our special offers. Write to us at the following address for information on our newest releases.

Harlequin Reader Service
U.S.: 3010 Walden Ave., P.O. Box 1325, Buffalo, NY 14269
Canadian: P.O. Box 609, Fort Erie, Ont. L2A 5X3

BABY BLUES
KRISTINE ROLOFSON

Harlequin Books

TORONTO • NEW YORK • LONDON
AMSTERDAM • PARIS • SYDNEY • HAMBURG
STOCKHOLM • ATHENS • TOKYO • MILAN
MADRID • WARSAW • BUDAPEST • AUCKLAND

To Glen, for the frozen cookies, warm socks and
twenty-four interesting years

ISBN 0-373-25594-2

BABY BLUES

1

"IT'S MY DESTINY," Martha McNally Winston informed her mother.

"Where did you get an idea like that?"

"Grandpa."

"I should have known." Anne took the folded newspaper her daughter was waving in front of her nose.

"There, under the What's Going On headline."

"'Auditions Wednesday and Thursday,'" Anne read out loud, "'from 7:00 to 10:00 at Matunuck Elementary School, for the summer season of Theater by the Sea. Children ages nine to eleven needed for this season's production of *The Music Man*. Bring photo.'" She handed the paper back to Martha. "What does this have to do with you?"

"This is Wednesday," the child declared, putting her hands on her hips. "I'm just the right age. I even look like I'm nine, if I put my hair in braids. And Grandpa says I sing like I'm thirty."

"So you think they're looking for a kid who looks young and sings old?" Anne knew Martha was an attractive child. She wore her brown hair long, blunt-cut to her shoulders, and her hazel eyes twinkled with good humor. When she smiled a dimple winked from her right cheek, but that was absolutely no reason for her to think about show business.

"Yep. And that's me."

"Oh, Martha," Anne began, wondering if she could discourage the child. Or, considering the past year, if she should. She wanted Martha to feel as if nothing was beyond her reach, so how could she say no to something the child wanted to try?

"Come on," Martha said. "I'll help you with the dishes so we can make the auditions by seven."

"I LOVE these auditions."

"Yeah, I know." Chris Bogart ran his hand through his dark hair and wondered how long he would have to endure another round of hopeful actors and actresses performing for him.

"All those beautiful women, singing, dancing, smiling at me," Denny stated with satisfaction.

"Wondering if sex will get them a part in the show," Chris Bogart added to his partner's list of audition actions.

"You have something against sex?"

"As currency, yes."

Denny laughed. "And they usually prefer you to me."

"I don't know why." Chris's looks had never made him stand out from the crowd, which was a drawback if you were an actor.

"Well, brace yourself, because we need a big cast for this show. Have you heard anything more from Johnny?"

Chris shook his head. "No. He's going to call when he knows if he can come. His agent is making noises for more money." He flipped to another page in his notebook. "What about our Marian the librarian?"

"Signed, sealed and scheduled to arrive—*with* her husband—next week. Helen helped her find a house to rent, but someone will have to pick them up at the train station."

"That shouldn't be a problem."

"The rest is wide open. Let's hope we have our Winthrop and Amaryllis out there." Denny looked at his watch. "Guess it's time to start this thing. We shouldn't have any trouble. Helen says the place is packed with kids."

"And we only need three." Chris grimaced. "And I'll bet the stage parents are out in force."

"Yeah."

"Well," Chris drawled, taking a seat at the end of the table, "I'm not putting up with parents who are a pain in the ass. I intend to meet the parents before we make any final decision on the child." The kid could have a show-stopping voice, but if the mother was an interfering maniac bitch from hell, then everyone backstage would suffer.

"You're in charge," Denny agreed.

Chris pulled a legal pad closer and nodded to the pianist. "Here we go. Tell Helen and Sal we're ready to roll."

SHE DIDN'T WANT to be here. She didn't want to watch her daughter, a hopeful expression on her heart-shaped face, hand her school photo to the woman behind the desk. She didn't want any part of show business. Yet here she was, sitting on a gray metal chair in the elementary school, waiting for Martha's name to be called. Waiting for Martha's hopes to be dashed.

"Boy, this feels good," her father said, rubbing his hands together.

"What does?" Anne was almost afraid to ask. Her father had retired when her mother had died. His heart hadn't been in show business any longer, he'd declared, and retired to Florida for nine months.

"This," he said, waving his arms wide. "It's good to be part of this again." Several people looked at him and smiled. The lobby was filled with people, all ages, shapes and sizes. Everyone except Anne hoped the producers would notice their talent and give them a part in one of the four musical productions for the summer season.

"I wish you hadn't encouraged Martha to do this."

"The child has a good voice, Annie. There's no reason—"

Martha returned to stand by her grandfather. "Aren't you trying out for anything, Grandpa?"

Dan McNally hesitated. "Audition? No, I've retired," he said with a sigh.

"That's right," Anne agreed. "Grandpa is retired now."

A sheepish expression crossed Dan's handsome face. "Maybe I could come out of retirement for the summer."

"What?"

"I think the theater is in my blood, honey."

Martha tugged at his hand. "You should try, Grandpa. They're still taking names and putting them down on the list," she informed him. "Too bad you didn't bring a song."

"Well," he said, his eyes twinkling, "I could just run back to the house and get my music, I suppose."

Anne shook her head and pulled the car keys from her purse. "Why am I not surprised that you brought it to Rhode Island with you?"

"I'd never go anywhere without my sheet music," he said, taking the keys. "Or my tap shoes. Or publicity photos." He looked thoughtful. "What song should I sing for the audition?"

Martha glanced down at her songbook. "I'm doing 'Somewhere Over the Rainbow.'"

"Yes," he agreed. "An excellent choice. Maybe I'll do one of my George Burns songs."

Anne closed her eyes and leaned back against the cement wall. Her head was starting to pound. Show business was in their blood, all right. It had to be hereditary. For a second Anne wondered if her life would have been easier if she'd been able to enjoy the odd, wandering life of her show-business parents.

"I'll put your name down," Martha said. "I think there are about fifty people ahead of me, so there's plenty of time."

"Well..." Dan hesitated. "They're doing four shows. Maybe there's a part for an old man in one of them. I believe the mayor in *The Music Man* is an excellent role."

"Sixty-seven isn't old," Anne said.

He grinned. "Never tell them your real age, darlin'." He winked at his granddaughter then, whistling the theme from *Oklahoma* as he went out the double doors to the parking lot.

"You okay, Mom?"

"I'm fine," she answered, without opening her eyes. "I've done this before." Yes, she decided, remembering. Life would definitely have been easier if she'd had some talent for singing or dancing or acting. Anything but a love of reading and an average skill with the piano. Her parents never believed she didn't have a drop of their talent. Surprisingly, the piano lessons had been the one thing Anne had enjoyed. Except when it came time to play in front of people.

What was she going to do with her father? Ten weeks ago he'd shown up on her doorstep, lonely for his only family and tired of Florida. As much as she loved him, she didn't have the faintest idea what would make him happy. And it was increasingly obvious he didn't know what to do with himself, either.

She'd been happy when he'd retired, thinking he'd finally decided to settle down in one place. Smell the flowers. Walk the beach.

And now, sing the songs.

An hour later Anne was still slumped on the same chair, when someone called, "Martha Winston!"

Dan patted her on the back, pushing her toward the door to the audition room at the same time. "Break a leg, baby."

"Good luck" was all that Anne could manage to say. The crowded room was filled with other hopeful children. Children with professional photographs and stage credits. She'd heard the mothers talking about New York agents and Boston's spring production of *Annie*. Anne looked at her watch. A few more minutes and this would be over. She could take Martha home, and with any luck the child would forget about show business.

Seven and a half minutes later Martha popped out of the room, a grin on her freckled face. "They want me to learn a dance. Can I stay?"

Anne nodded numbly. "Okay." Martha went back inside the room, and several women shot Anne an envious glance.

Dan rubbed his hands together. "That's a good sign. A *very* good sign."

That was a matter of opinion. She didn't want Martha in show business, not even in a local summer theater half a mile from the house. She didn't want her daughter to have the life she'd had. "I'm not sure about this," she muttered.

"Lighten up, Annie-girl."

Anne groaned. Why was she here? Because her dear sweet father hadn't looked so happy since Edie had died, and it had broken her heart to see him grieve for so long. The old spark was back, not as strong, but certainly flickering valiantly.

If these ridiculous auditions helped, then she'd sit here on this torturous metal chair the entire evening. Even though it was a school night, and she'd acted as substitute teacher for high-school English classes all day. With only two weeks of school left, teaching on any grade level or subject was difficult.

"Number sixty-one, Dan McNally!"

"Knock 'em dead, Daddy," Anne said as her father gathered his sheet music and started toward the audition room, which was actually the tiny elementary-school recreation room.

When he returned, he grinned at his daughter.

"How did it go?" she whispered, conscious of the curious looks some of the other people gave them.

Dan reclaimed the seat beside her. "It went well," he said. "Of course, you never know what they're looking for. Is Marty still in the running?"

"As far as I know. I had hoped to have her in bed by now."

"What's wrong with her having a part in the show? It's a nice atmosphere."

"I guess I don't understand the attraction. Why can't she just be a normal kid and spend the summer riding her bike to the beach?"

He shook his head. "What's wrong with her using the talent God gave her—and she inherited from her grandfather?"

"The 'smell of the greasepaint, the roar of the crowd' kind of thing?"

"There's no business—"

"Like show business," she finished for him. "I've heard that before."

"Your mother could sing the heck out of that song."

They were both silent, remembering Edie's knack for belting out a show-stopping tune.

"And now little Martha is following in her grandmother's footsteps." Dan sighed.

"Maybe," Anne cautioned. She looked around the room, encouraged by the numbers of waiting children. Surely the odds were against Martha McNally Winston making her entrance into show business this summer.

Dan cleared his throat. "You'll never guess who I ran into, Annie. You should—"

"Mrs. Winston?" A young woman stepped through the crowd.

Anne raised her hand and stood. "That's me."

"Could you come in here for a minute, please? The producers would like to talk to you."

"All right." She looked at her father and he gave her the thumbs-up sign, but he appeared worried. Anne ignored the curious stares from the crowd and followed the thin woman in the black leotard into the recreation room.

A curly-haired young man seated in the middle of the long table piled with photographs and yellow legal pads stood up and held out his hand.

"Hi. I'm Denny Mitchell," he said with a practiced smile. "The producer."

"Anne Winston," she said, glancing toward Martha, who was perched on a stool by the school piano with another man and the accompanist. "The mother."

The two young women sitting on either side of Denny smiled.

The tall man standing by the piano gave Martha some sheet music and a quick pat on the shoulder. "You did a great job" she heard him say in a deep voice.

That was nice of him, Anne thought as Denny said, "Chris, here's Martha's mother."

He looked up, in the middle of a smile. Tall, lean and excruciatingly familiar, he walked over to Anne and held out his hand. "Hello," he said, waiting for her to accept his handshake.

"Hello," she echoed. She quickly gave him her hand and just as quickly took it back. He didn't recognize her. But she knew him, would know him anywhere. He hadn't changed much since he'd walked out of her life twelve years ago. He looked the same, with the lean face, the expressive brown eyes and especially the dark curling hair and mouth full of killer white teeth. Expensive teeth. And lips that kissed with the most alarming skill.

He appeared puzzled for a second, then gave Martha an encouraging glance as she hopped off the stool and stood beside him. He turned back to Anne. "Your daughter has quite a powerful voice, Ms. Winston."

"Yes" was all she could manage to say. This couldn't really be happening, not now, not like this.

He nodded. "We won't be making any final decisions today for casting *The Music Man*, but I need to know if she would be available for three weeks of rehearsals June 21 to July 19, then the show." He glanced down at his clipboard. "It starts July 20 and runs for four weeks. Two shows on Saturday night, with matinees on Thursdays, and Mondays off. You need to consider whether or not you and Martha can handle that kind of schedule and if it interferes with any summer plans you may have."

"I'll give it some thought." Thank God, he didn't know who she was. He didn't remember that summer, which really shouldn't surprise her. It was just one of those summer romances, destined to dissolve at the first hint of autumn. She'd survived. Barely, but she'd survived. And that's what counted.

"We're not going on vacation," Martha offered. "We can't afford it this year."

Anne frowned. Next thing she knew Martha would be telling him how much money they had in the bank.

"If she gets the part, I'll be in touch within the week."

"What part are you talking about?" She didn't know where the ability to ask an intelligent question came from, but she was grateful her voice sounded natural.

"Amaryllis. She sings 'Good Night, My Someone' in the first act. Aside from the solo, she has quite a few lines to learn."

Martha grinned. "I'm good at memorizing."

"That's good to know," Denny said.

Chris thanked Martha for coming and then Denny ushered them out the door. Once in the hall, Anne let out the breath she'd been holding. He hadn't recognized her, of that she was certain.

He hadn't remembered her as the nineteen-year-old who'd thought she was in love with him one summer many, many years ago. Her hair wasn't streaked with blond, straight with thick bangs that covered her eyebrows. She didn't weigh one hundred and one pounds anymore, and she no longer had stars in her eyes.

A failed marriage and single motherhood certainly took care of the stars.

She didn't believe in starry-eyed romance anymore, either. Especially summer romances with overly good-looking actors.

If he didn't remember her, he would soon. He'd eventually remember Dan McNally starring in the 1981 summer season. Daddy had drawn rave reviews in *Guys and Dolls* and *Yankee Doodle Dandy*. Chris had played smaller parts, but his good looks and comedic talent had caught an agent's eye and by the end of August he was on his way to fame and fortune.

Anne was on her way back to college and the maternity ward at South County Hospital.

She ushered Martha through the crowd to her waiting grandfather. The worried expression in his eyes didn't ease as she attempted a smile.

"I tried to warn you," he murmured.

"It's okay," she lied. "It's really okay."

ANNE MCNALLY. Correction. Anne Winston, with a child. A child who sang like Ethel Merman and Kate Smith rolled into one little four-foot-nine-inch package. First he'd had the pleasant surprise of seeing Dan McNally again—older, but with the same booming voice and professional bearing—and ready to trot the boards. The old charmer would be an asset in any production. Too bad the part of Mayor Shinn had been cast in New York.

Denny tapped Martha's school photo. "Looks like we've found our Amaryllis."

"Maybe."

"Maybe? The kid's perfect!"

"She should be. After all, she's Dan McNally's granddaughter." Chris noted the blank expression on his partner's face. "You're too young to remember. He's an old pro. He and his wife probably performed on every stage in the States and plenty overseas."

"Didn't we just audition him?"

Chris nodded. "Until he walked in here today I thought he was dead or had retired to a condo somewhere."

"Martha's mother seemed sane enough."

"Martha's mother?" He thought of her long waving hair and those hazel eyes that watched him with a completely unreadable expression. She'd gotten better at hiding her feelings. He used to be able to look in her eyes and know exactly what she was thinking.

"An attractive woman," Denny noted. "Think she'll turn into a dragon backstage?"

"Annie? No." Not the Annie he'd known so well. She'd been sweet and kind, a little bit shy at the age of nineteen. Of course, he'd been a man of the world at twenty-two, having obtained his first real acting job since graduating from college.

"Chris?"

"What?"

"Can we call in the next one?"

He tapped his papers against his palm. "Yeah." He went around the table and sat down. He hadn't thought about Anne in years. He'd never known what had happened to her. She must have gone to school as she'd planned, married someone with a business degree, no doubt. Someone who wore suits to work and brought home a steady paycheck every other week. She'd wanted a home and security, and he was sure she'd gotten exactly what she'd wanted.

Well, he hoped she was happy. Had she recognized him? He'd bet the closing night receipts that she had, but if she wanted to pretend they'd never met, had never made love, then he would go along with it. He didn't question why it annoyed him so much. He broke his pencil in half and tossed it aside.

"Chris?"

He grimaced. "I'm just tired," he explained, and leaned back in his chair as a well-endowed redhead, her dancer's body encased in a tight black catsuit, bounced toward the table. Her overly bright smile revealed perfect teeth framed with red lipstick.

"Hi!" She handed her photo to Denny and extended her hand to Chris. "I'm Candy Barrett, and I'm going to sing a medley from *Cats*." She handed her music to the pianist and then took several deep breaths as the opening bars of the music sounded.

Chris composed his features into polite attention. God save him from actresses.

"Ms. WINSTON? This is Chris Bogart, at Theater by the Sea."

As if she wouldn't know his voice. "Oh. Hello."

"We'd like to see Martha again," he said. "Could you bring her to the theater this afternoon so we can audition her with the lead actress?"

"Are you sure?"

There was a moment of silence, as if he hadn't expected the question. "Are you?"

Anne stared at the package of hamburger on the counter and thought of the past days of listening to the music from *The Music Man*. "Yes, I suppose so." *And we've got trouble right here in River City.* "She doesn't get home from school until after three."

"That's fine. How does four o'clock sound?"

"All right."

"Good. See you then."

Anne hung up the phone. She didn't know who was going to be more excited, her father or her daughter. The good thing was that she'd talked to Chris Bogart without sounding like an idiot.

"'Seventy-six trombones,'" Dan sang, on his way into the kitchen. "What's the matter, darlin'?"

If she heard "Seventy-six Trombones" again, she would scream so loud that seventy-seven trombones couldn't drown out the sound. "Chris Bogart called. He wants Martha to come back and sing again."

"Well, she's ready," Dan stated with glee.

He had rented *The Music Man* from the video store, instructing his granddaughter on the importance of studying for a part. Martha had been practicing hitting the high notes on "her" song. Anne hadn't realized her daughter had such a powerful voice. Actually, she'd always known it was loud; she just hadn't realized it was on key.

"It's not her I'm worried about." She dumped the two pounds of ground beef into a bowl and began assembling the ingredients for a meat loaf.

"Don't you want her to be happy?"

"Don't ask me to explain it. I just don't like it. That's all."

Dan sighed. "You don't have to explain it, Annie-girl. I have two eyes, y'know, and a rather clever brain at times."

"What do you mean, Daddy?" She stuck the wooden spoon into the bowl of meat-loaf mixture and beat it as if mixing it together would solve all her problems.

"Your mother and I knew good and well who Martha's father had to be," he began, lowering his deep voice to a whisper. "But we kept quiet, which may or may not have been the best thing."

"I don't want to discuss this," she said, staring down at the bowl of ground meat.

"You never have," he replied. "And I respect that. But if you ever want to talk about what's botherin' you, I'm here. This old hoofer had better be good for something."

She looked over at him and smiled. "Thanks, Daddy. For now, let's just say I don't want Martha in show business. I want her to be a *normal* kid."

He shook his head. "She misses her friends in California and she's lonely. She worries about you, and even if John wasn't the greatest father, Marty still misses having a man around the house."

"At least she has you now."

"She's happy about this opportunity, Annie. Let her enjoy it. If she gets it, she'll feel like she belongs somewhere."

"And what if she doesn't get the part?"

He shrugged. "We'll do something together, like singing lessons or dancing lessons. And there's always another part, another show."

"Show-business optimism again."

Dan winked. "In this business, what else is there?"

Anne readied everything for dinner while she waited for Martha to come home from school. After she told her she was expected at the theater at four o'clock, she added, "Are you sure you want to do this?"

Martha twirled around the kitchen and shrieked with excitement. It didn't look as if Martha could be talked out of doing the show.

After she stopped giggling, Martha looked incredulous. "How can you say that?"

"I just thought—"

"Mom! I've been dreaming of this. I've been practicing with Grandpa all week. And I almost have the part!" Her little face lit up with happiness. She looked as though she'd just won an Academy Award.

"If you're sure . . ." Anne didn't have the heart to say no, although she thought it might be a good idea. After all, the divorce had been especially difficult for Martha. Moving to a new state and a new school had added to the child's feelings that she didn't belong anywhere.

"Can we practice before we go?"

Anne relented, and went to the piano. She ran through the chords, gave Martha her opening note, then began the song. Martha opened her mouth and let the words pour out.

"YOUR GRANDDAUGHTER? I should have known. Something about that voice was familiar," Chris said, shaking Dan's hand.

"She's a chip off the old block," Dan said. He turned to Anne. "Isn't she, Annie?"

"Of course." In many ways.

"You remember Annie," Dan prompted. "'Course, that was twelve years ago, and we were all a lot younger then."

"I knew who she was right away," he said. "She hasn't changed at all."

Then Chris smiled, a warm inviting smile that made Anne think of long, private hours in the dunes of Moonstone Beach. Her stomach flipped alarmingly.

"I didn't think you recognized me." Anne struggled to banish the disturbing memories and concentrate on why she was standing there in the middle of the damp lobby. "After all, it's been quite a few years."

"Too many. I didn't think you remembered me, either."

Anne realized he might have felt as awkward as she did last Wednesday evening. Besides, the middle of auditions wasn't the perfect place to hold a private reunion.

"We'll have to catch up on old times," he said smoothly.

"Sure." *I'll make a coffee cake and tell you that you're the father of an eleven-year-old girl. Should be fun.*

"Hi, Mr. Bogart." Martha moved through the lobby and peered through the doorway toward the stage.

"Hi, Martha. Becky, our lead, should be along in a minute," Chris said. "She plays the librarian. Are you familiar with the play?"

Martha nodded. "I've seen the movie a few times."

"Good. I want you to read for the part of Amaryllis, just like you did last week. Then you and Becky will sing some of the song 'Good Night, My Someone' together."

"Okay." Martha grinned up at him. She'd insisted Anne braid her long dark hair into two plaits on either side of her head, and she wore soft denim overalls and a paisley shirt because Anne had refused to buy her a calico dress, the kind Amaryllis had worn in the movie. Thick pink ankle socks and clean tennis shoes completed the outfit.

She was more like her grandfather every day.

Chris eyed her approvingly. "You look good," he told her, as if he knew it had taken her over an hour to achieve the appearance of a turn-of-the-century child.

Anne glanced back and forth between the two of them. She couldn't see any resemblance. Martha was pure McNally, right down to her delicate bone structure and tiny feet. The dark hair was the identical shade of Chris's, but that was the only similarity.

No one would ever know. And even if Martha told him how old she was, he could simply assume Anne had met someone after school started. A man like Chris Bogart would be too busy to discover a child's birthdate and start counting on his fingers.

The kid was a charmer. A natural one, which was rare. She reminded him of her grandmother. From what he could remember of Edie McNally, she'd been a live wire, just like her husband. The two of them had had a reputation in the theater world for professionalism and enthusiasm. They'd been kind to a kid just starting out, and he'd never forgotten it.

Chris forced himself to concentrate on the audition. Denny was supposed to be here with the accompanist, but he was late as usual. In the meantime Becky pretended to play the piano, and she and Martha practiced their lines.

Chris looked at his watch. "I'm sorry about this delay. The pianist was supposed to be here half an hour ago."

"Anne could play for you," Dan offered. He sat comfortably in third row center as if he owned the theater. "Go ahead, Anne. Help the man out."

Chris glanced over at her. "I didn't know you played."

"Not very well," she said.

"Nonsense," said her father. "She's been my rehearsal accompanist for years."

Anne shot him a helpless look and stood up. "All right, if it will help." *If it will get me out of here faster.*

Chris led her to a piano offstage. "I appreciate this," he said, his hand on her arm to guide her through the small, crowded area. "Watch it," he cautioned. "We're setting up for next week's opening of *The Odd Couple.*"

She sat down on the bench and ran her fingers along the keys, then tried a few chords. Her arm was warm where his fingers had touched her skin.

"We just had it tuned," he said.

"Yes." She waited, then said, "Do you have the music?"

He looked down at the papers in his hand, then handed them to her. "It starts when Amaryllis says, 'May I play my . . .' etc., etc."

Anne flipped through the pages and found it. She placed the music on the stand and practiced the opening a few times before turning back to Chris. "All set."

"All right." He went onto the stage and spoke to Becky and Martha. At his nod, Anne started the song.

Their voices blended beautifully—Becky's strong, vibrant soprano and Martha's pure, unpracticed voice combined in a touching rendition of the romantic song. A few seconds of silence followed the song, and Becky eyed Chris with raised eyebrows.

Too much of a professional to interfere with the casting of the show, Becky gave Martha a hug. "Where did you learn to sing like that?"

Martha shrugged. "I don't know. It just comes out."

"It's in her blood," Dan announced proudly.

Anne winced, then came from backstage and put the sheet music on top of the piano.

"Thank you, Martha," Chris said, coming over to the stage. "You did a great job."

Martha slid off the piano stool and grinned. "Don't call us, we'll call you?"

Chris smiled. "Something like that. There are other children coming back to sing tonight, and we'll make our decision tomorrow." He looked over at Anne. "Thanks for coming," he said. "And thanks for the help with the music."

"You're welcome." She wanted to take Martha's hand and drag her out of the theater while there was still time to get away. Chris couldn't fool her. She'd sat through enough auditions to know when the producer or director was impressed. The one called Denny sat in the back row and gave Becky the thumbs-up sign.

Chris Bogart had found his Amaryllis. Anne was happy for Martha, but how would she keep Chris from knowing he'd also found a daughter?

He might offer Martha the part, but that didn't mean she was going to take it. After all, she was still the mother around here, show business or not. So why did she feel that the summer was slowly spinning out of control?

CHRIS LISTENED to the others. Adam Brock, an appealing little boy with a charming way of imitating a lisp, was his choice for the part of Winthrop, Marian's shy little brother with the speech impediment. The kid had never danced before, but Bryan, the choreographer, assured him that Adam could learn the steps of the dances. He'd managed to pick it up on Thursday's auditions. One of the little girls, the one with the frizzy blond hair, would be perfect for the mayor's youngest daughter. The mayor and his wife had been cast out of New York, which left the dancers. The part of the constable would go to Dan McNally, if he'd accept a small part and a few lines.

Something told him that Dan wasn't going to be fussy. Besides, how could Anne refuse to let Martha be in the play if the child's grandfather was going to be there, too?

And he very much wanted Martha in the play. He didn't stop to question all the reasons why.

2

"ANNE?"

"Yes?"

"This is Chris Bogart again. We'd like Martha to play Amaryllis."

Anne pressed the phone closer to her ear. When her father watched the news he turned the television volume high enough to be heard throughout the house. "You would?"

"Yes. We've all agreed that she has the right look for the part, and her voice has blown everyone away. Becky hasn't stopped talking about her. So, what do you say?"

Anne took a deep breath. She could say no, and Martha would never have to know that the role had been offered to her. But she couldn't do that to her daughter. She'd never been much of a liar, and she couldn't start now. She would protect Martha with her life, but she knew she couldn't deny her this chance. "All right."

There was a brief silence. "Yesterday your father told me he wasn't sure you'd let her do this," he said finally. "What made you say yes?"

She tried to answer as honestly as she could without revealing anything too personal. "Martha's had a rough year. This is the first thing she's shown an interest in for quite a while."

"I'm glad. She seems like a great kid and I know she'll do well."

The warmth in his voice threatened to undo her composure. He thought Martha was a great kid.

He continued. "There'll be a cast meeting before the first rehearsal on Tuesday, June 22, at nine o'clock. Our rehearsal hall is in Wakefield, on Woodruff Avenue. It's a big building behind the bike shop."

"I know where it is."

"If you and your husband would come here to the theater tomorrow, we can discuss the financial arrangements. I'll be here all day, so anytime is all right."

"That's fine. I'll come by in the morning." She didn't want to tell him there was no husband. She didn't want to share anything personal with him. All she could hope was that she could keep this on a strictly business level, and yet there was so much more to this than she wanted to think about. A few days ago life had seemed so simple. Why did she have to have a kid who read the newspaper?

"Good. I'll see you tomorrow then."

"Thanks for calling. Martha's going to be thrilled." This was very civilized, as if they hadn't slept together so many times so many years ago. Maybe he'd forgotten. She hoped so, and yet she knew she'd hate the thought of him forgetting what they'd shared that summer.

"Don't hang up yet. I'd like to talk to your father, too, if he's there."

"He's here. Just a minute." She was relieved to be able to put the phone down. "Dad," she called, stepping into the doorway that separated the tiny kitchen from the living room that ran the front length of the house. He sat in the big blue recliner she'd bought for him, the remote control in his hand as he stared at the news. "Dad," she tried again.

"What?"

"Phone for you. Chris Bogart," she said, watching his face light up. "Martha got the part of Amaryllis."

He hopped out of the chair and did a two-step on the braided rug. "'Happy days are here again,'" he hummed.

"Now he wants to talk to you," Anne reminded him. He did his dance from the living room right through the door to the kitchen and the counter where the phone lay.

"Christopher? Hello!"

Anne watched from the doorway, her fingers crossed behind her back. If he could just get some kind of part in one of the shows, he might just start feeling better. Grief had taken its toll on Danny McNally, and Anne hated to see her father so depressed. Since the audition, he'd seemed more like his old self, even though the sadness crossed his face all too often.

"Fine, fine," he said, drumming his fingers on the counter. "No, I don't mind at all." He turned to Anne and winked. "We'll have a good time. Okay, thanks. See you then."

He hung up the phone and grinned at Anne. "I got the part of the constable."

"Does the constable sing and dance?"

His smile grew wider. "Of course. Can you stand having two actors in the family?"

"I'm used to it," she drawled. "Just tell me I'm doing the right thing."

He held out his arms and Anne went into his embrace. "What makes Martha happy has got to be the right thing."

"But what if—"

"Shh," he admonished. "'What will be will be.'"

"Stop that."

"Stop what?"

"Talking in songs," she murmured, grateful for the strong arms of her father around her.

He chuckled. "An old habit, Annie-girl. Used to drive your mother crazy."

"I remember."

"She'd like this," he declared. "Me and Martha, on the same stage."

"'There's no business like show business.'"

"It's in the blood," her father repeated, and this time his voice was serious. "You should know that better than anyone."

"Don't start with me, Daddy."

He ignored her order. "I was wrong, you know."

"About what?"

"That fall, when you told us you were pregnant. I was wrong when I told you to forget him, whoever he was. You should have told Chris the truth, that he was going to be a father."

"He was halfway around the world."

Dan stepped back, forcing Anne to look up at him. "He's right down the street now," he said. "And it's never too late."

Anne shook her head. "I wish that were true, but it's too late for a lot of things."

"Not something as important as this."

Her father put into words what she herself knew. Chris deserved the truth, even after all of these years. "I know you're right, but I don't want Martha to be hurt. I don't know what kind of man Chris is, or even that he cares that he has a child. For all I know, he could have lots of children. He could be married."

"I doubt it."

"Why?"

Her father shrugged. "Just a hunch."

"I'm supposed to meet with him tomorrow."

"You're going to have to tell him sometime, Annie. A secret like that can't—shouldn't—be kept forever."

"I know, Daddy. I'm just not ready. I can't let Martha be hurt."

"You have the next seven weeks to make sure that doesn't happen."

A COLLEGE-AGED WOMAN at the ticket window told her to go upstairs, so Anne went through the wide red doors and into the lobby. Another young woman, busy arranging photographs on the bulletin board, smiled at Anne as she hesitated in front of the display. The glitter-coated letters announced that *The Odd Couple* was about to open Theater by the Sea's new summer season.

Anne turned to go upstairs to the balcony. It was eerie being back in the historic old theater. The weathered shingled building had been a theater since the early 1930s, she remembered her father saying. Climbing the narrow staircase she couldn't believe that twelve years had passed since she'd been inside.

And it was an even stranger feeling knowing she was going to meet Chris here. She'd thought he'd be on Broadway by now, his name in lights, adoring women at his feet. Well, she didn't know about the lights, but she knew there were plenty of women. There was never any shortage of beautiful women in show business, and twelve summers ago Chris had attracted his share.

He'd wanted only her. Or so he'd said.

The balcony smelled of lemon oil and freshly cut lumber. On her left were the balcony seats. A young man, his body hooked in a precarious position from the ceiling, moved the lights while a man on stage called directions. On her right was a white door marked Private, so she knocked. No one answered, but she heard rock music and voices, so she opened the door a few inches.

"Hello?"

Chris looked up from leaning over a drafting table. His smile threatened to take her breath away, and she hoped she didn't seem like one of those star-struck women she was certain he was accustomed to talking with.

"Come in, Anne," he said, moving toward her. He took her hand as if they'd been together forever and led her to the young man seated at the drafting board. "Meet Pete, resident set designer," he said.

The young man grinned, long hair curling down to his shoulders. His red bandanna lent him a rakish air. He couldn't have been more than twenty-five.

"Hi."

"Anne is an old friend of mine, and her daughter is our Amaryllis in *The Music Man*."

"It's nice to meet you," she said, pulling her hand away from Chris's grasp as soon as she could without being rude. His easy assumption of their friendship surprised her. Friends. There was nothing the least bit threatening in that word, so why didn't she believe it could be possible?

"Here," he said, pulling out a chair near a desk piled high with papers. He reached over to the radio and turned the volume down. "Have a seat."

"All right." She hadn't known what to wear. Jeans seemed too casual, and appearing in a dress might be interpreted as trying to impress him. She'd settled for a loose flowered sundress, the kind where you could be eight months pregnant and no one would be able to tell.

Chris sat behind his desk and explained how the company handled hiring children, and when he was finished Anne was satisfied Martha would be well looked after. The financial arrangements were made, the papers signed and the forms filled out. Martha's birthdate was listed on several forms, and Anne held her breath as Chris stood with the information in his hands. He didn't glance at anything but her signature.

"You said she'll do eight shows a week?" she repeated, hoping to distract him.

He tucked the papers in a manila folder and put it on a stack of similar folders on the corner of his desk. "Two evening performances on Saturday, matinee on Thursday," he explained. "The cast is off on Mondays, and the show runs for four weeks." He smiled again. "We expect it to be our hit of the season. The sales are already ahead of last year, which is a relief."

"How long have you owned the theater?"

"Three years. This is our third season."

"Do you have a part in any of the shows?"

"You mean onstage?" He shook his head. "No, I like producing and directing."

"I'm surprised. I thought you would always be an actor."

Chris leaned back in his chair. "I did, but more and more the backstage work appealed to me. When the opportunity came to buy this place my friends and I sank every dime we had into it. We've done quite a bit of renovation, too. Would you like a tour?"

She looked at her watch and stood up. "I really have to go."

"What are you doing here in Matunuck, Annie?" He glanced down at her hand. "Are you married? You're not wearing a wedding ring, and you haven't mentioned your husband."

"I'm divorced. My ex-husband lives in San Diego." Careful statements, she realized, unwilling to further the lie.

"What made you come back here? Was it because Dan retired here?"

"No. I went to college in Rhode Island, remember?" She waited for his nod. "I always liked the area, so when it came time to change my life, this was the first place I thought of. We bought a little house down the street. Dan grew tired of retirement in Florida a few months ago and came up here to visit. He'd liked it so much he stayed."

"He must have been lonely."

"Very. He hasn't been the same since my mother died."

"I was sorry to hear about that."

"Thank you."

She took a step backward, hoping he'd take the hint, but he ignored her move. He leaned forward, as if he wanted answers to his questions before he would let her leave the tiny office. "What do you do here, Anne?"

"I substitute-teach at the junior high and high school. I'm trying to get a full-time teaching position in town, but it's not easy. In fact, I have an interview today."

"Good luck," and he sounded as if he meant it. "Knock 'em dead."

"Show-business talk again."

He shrugged. "What else is there?"

"Normalcy," she replied. "Early bedtimes and music on the radio and a steady paycheck at the end of the week."

He didn't smile as he stood and came round the desk to stand close to her. "Still the same Annie, I see. Still wanting to know what's around the bend before you set foot on the road."

She shrugged. "I don't like to take chances."

"I know," he said heavily.

"What about you, Chris? Are you married?"

"Not anymore."

"No children?"

His smile was wry. "No. Why?"

"I just wondered." *Just wondered if Martha had brothers and sisters.* "You seem good with kids."

"I've worked with a lot of them. Most of them were great, or would have been if their parents hadn't interfered."

She backed toward the door. "I'll try not to be a stereotypical stage mother, but I want to make sure Martha will be all right."

"We'll take good care of her. Parents aren't allowed backstage during the shows, but you'll receive complimentary tickets for opening night, and we'll try to make the entire process as painless as possible."

"Thank you. I know I'll be a wreck."

"Her grandfather will take good care of her, and so will I."

For some reason, she believed him. "Well, I have to go."

"Anne."

She turned around, her hand on the doorknob. "Yes?"

"Friday night is the opening for *The Odd Couple*. Would you like to come?"

"Well, I—"

"It's press night, so we like to have the house as full as possible. Would you be my guest?"

She hesitated. She didn't want to be rude, and she'd love to see the play. "All right," she said.

"Would you mind meeting me here around seven-thirty? We can have a drink before the show starts. I won't be able to leave to come pick you up."

"I live close to here. It's no problem."

"I'll take you home."

"You don't have to."

"I want to." He ran his hand through his hair. "We haven't even gone out yet and we're already arguing."

"We're not arguing," she protested.

"I'll wait for you on the front porch."

"Okay," she agreed. They used to meet in the back of the theater, by the stairs to the staff quarters. A huge lilac bush had hidden their kisses from everyone else, or so she'd thought.

She escaped from the office and headed to her car. After a conversation with Chris Bogart, the job interview at the high school would be easy.

"WELL, HE DIDN'T waste any time," her father said, sprawled in his recliner. Martha lay near his feet, a row of cards spread out in front of her on the beige carpet.

"Who?" Martha asked.

Anne shook her head at her father. "No one," she replied.

Martha grinned. "Chris Bogart, right?"

"Right," her grandfather answered. "She's going out with him tonight."

"I'm not going out with him. It's press night at the theater. I'm going to fill a seat, that's all."

"And fill it very prettily, too," her father said, winking at her. "I've always liked you in green."

Anne glanced down at her sage-green sheath. Straight from her shoulders to above her knees, it was a simple dress, although stockings and pumps dressed it up. She wore gold hoop earrings and her hair fell to her shoulders in soft waves. She'd taken time with her makeup, making sure she appeared her best.

"You're wearing the bracelet," Dan said, pleased.

Her parents had given her a diamond tennis bracelet when she'd graduated from college, but she hadn't had many opportunities to wear it lately. "For courage," she explained.

"You don't need courage," Dan said. "You're a beautiful woman."

"You look *great*," Martha added. "Even if you don't have a real date."

"Thanks." She glanced at the clock on the video recorder. "Dad, would you drive me down there? I was going to walk, but I don't want to be late."

He hopped out of the chair. "Of course, darlin'. You look too good to be walking down the street," he replied.

She told herself she could handle this. After all, she would be seeing Chris for the next six weeks or so. It would be easier if her stomach didn't knot up every time she looked at him. He was still as handsome as ever.

She noticed him right away. Standing on the front porch, he appeared elegant and confident in a black tuxedo as he talked with a crowd of people. Her father pulled the car up to the front, and Anne stepped out onto the gravel area in front of the steps.

"Have a good time," Dan said. "I was Oscar one season," he said. "It's a great role."

"I'll think of you," she promised.

"We won't wait up," he said, winking.

She shut the door. "I won't be late."

"Yes, you will," a man's voice said.

Anne turned to see Chris standing behind her on the last step of the wide stairs to the porch.

"I guarantee it."

She wished he didn't take her breath away, wished she could think of something clever to say. Other than "Hi," which was the best she could do.

He stepped onto the gravel and took her elbow. "You look beautiful," he said.

"Thank you." She let him guide her toward the gazebo, where blue-shirted young men served drinks in plastic champagne glasses.

"Champagne," he said to one of the bartenders, and then handed Anne a glass full of the sparkling liquid. Taking one himself, Chris glanced down at her and smiled. "To a successful evening," he said, touching her glass with his.

"To rave reviews," she added, taking a sip of the cold champagne.

"Yes." He grimaced. "The critics are here, with their pads and pencils, ready to pass judgment."

"How can you go wrong with Neil Simon?"

"You can't," he said. "Which is why Denny suggested it in the first place. Now we have to see if he's right." He led her away from the crowd. "Come on, I'd like you to meet some of the people who work here."

"Aren't you nervous?"

"Terrified," he admitted. "We need a strong opener for the season. The dress rehearsal went pretty well, and the actors have had a chance to speed things up a bit. It's flowing better now."

Knots of people gathered in the grassy area between the theater and the rear building, where a trellis-covered walkway led to the restaurant and lounge.

"It looks so different from what I remember," Anne said, following him across the grass.

"We've put a lot of money into the grounds," Chris explained, touching her elbow to guide her toward the porch. "We plan to add more shrubbery every year."

"It's lovely." Anne took another sip of champagne. This was actually going well. Twelve years ago they would have had each other's clothes off by now. It was good to know a person could grow up and act civilized, conduct polite conversation about gardens and business.

If he would only stop touching her. His hand had moved from her elbow to her back as they climbed the steps.

"Denny," he said to a familiar-looking man with curly blond hair and round-rimmed glasses. "You remember Anne Winston from the auditions?"

"Of course. Martha's mother." He shook her hand. "Good. You have champagne. Obviously Chris is taking good care of you this evening."

"Yes. I'm looking forward to the show."

He grimaced and fingered the collar of his shirt. "I hope it goes well. Press night, you know. The only time I'm forced to wear a tux."

"I'll keep my fingers crossed."

Denny lifted his glass and finished his drink. "Is it about time, Chris?"

He looked at his watch. "Ten minutes."

"An eternity," Denny growled, as Chris chuckled. "Guess I'd better go mingle with the press a little longer."

"There are quite a few of them over by the bar," Chris said. "Anne and I are going to find seats."

"See you later, Anne. Enjoy the show."

"Enjoy the show," an attractive woman with short silver hair repeated as she handed Anne a program. Dressed in a silk pink blouse and khaki cotton skirt, she didn't look like an usher, until Anne realized that the other ushers wore the same color combination.

"Marie, I'd like you to meet a friend of mine, Anne Winston. Anne, this is Marie Jameson."

"It's nice to meet you," Anne said, noting the woman's friendly smile.

"I've heard so much about you and your father. And I'm anxious to meet that talented daughter of yours. *The Music Man* will be a popular show."

"I hope so, for Chris's sake," Anne murmured politely.

"How are we doing, Marie?"

"They're trickling in."

"It's about time to ring the bell." He looked at his watch again. "I'll tell T.J."

"Enjoy your evening, Anne. It was nice meeting you."

"You'll be seeing a lot of Anne," Chris promised.

Of course, Anne told herself, he meant because Martha was in *The Music Man*. He couldn't mean anything else.

Anne told herself she had to remember that this was a simple evening out, not a date with a man she used to love. She wasn't supposed to enjoy Chris sitting next to her in the dark, the smell of his after-shave or the simple pleasure of a male body seated so close to her. They sat in the last row, which contained various people associated with the theater, since they knew one another's names and whispered of calamities backstage. Off to one side a man operated a board full of switches and colored lights. Denny slid next to Chris and whispered that he was going upstairs to watch the show from the balcony.

When the curtain rose on the first act, the audience applauded, and Chris leaned back in his seat. At one point he made an automatic motion, as if to take her hand, then stopped and clutched the arms of the seat instead.

Thank goodness he hadn't held her hand. She might have done something foolish, like enjoy it.

3

HE COULDN'T BELIEVE he'd almost reached for her hand. Thank God he'd caught himself in time. It was only instinctive, he told himself, to reach for a hand to hold as the curtain went up on his business. On his life. It was only natural he should need a little moral support.

He'd gripped the armrests instead. The first act went smoothly and by the time the lights were turned up for intermission, he was ready for a break. He felt as if he'd been holding his breath the entire time.

"It was wonderful," she said. "Can you relax now?"

Chris turned to her and shrugged. "Maybe for a few minutes. Are you enjoying it?"

"Very much. It's very professional. I don't think you have anything to worry about. When do the reviews come out?"

"The *Providence Journal* is Tuesday, the *Narragansett Times* on Wednesday. There are others, but those are the two that matter the most. If the reviews are good, sales should take off."

"I remember my parents waiting up all night for the reviews in the morning editions."

"In New York?"

"Yes."

She'd matured from a pretty girl to a beautiful woman, he realized. But that shouldn't have surprised him. "I remember..." he began.

Dennis tapped him on the shoulder. "The first act is still too slow."

Chris reluctantly turned around. "Yes, but it's better than it was two days ago."

Dennis nodded, a grim expression on his face until he looked at Anne. "What do you think, Anne?"

"I'm enjoying it," she answered. "And I've been watching people as they walk by. They're smiling. That's always a good sign, don't you think?"

"Since you're an expert," Chris said. "We'll agree with you."

"I didn't say I was an expert."

"Bet you can't count the number of opening nights you've attended."

She shook her head. "I hate to ruin my status as an expert, but most of them I was too young to remember, and certainly not old enough to have opinions on the show." She smiled. "Although, now that I think of it, my parents always asked me what I thought. Of course, they knew I'd tell them they were wonderful."

"That's good enough for us," Dennis assured her, leaving his perch on the arm of the end seat. "We'll be glad to believe anything you say."

"As long as it's good," Chris added, turning back to her as Dennis slipped into the lobby.

"Don't let me stop you from mingling."

"More like pacing," he said. "I was going to offer you a drink." *I was going to tell you I remembered the first time I saw you.* "What would you like? Another glass of champagne?"

"I'd like that."

"You used to drink ginger ale."

"I still do, but how did you remember that?"

"I remember a lot of things," he said, and watched her cheeks turn pink. He shouldn't have teased her, he realized, and hurried to add, "Like the book you were reading when I first saw you and those short denim shorts you used to wear."

"*Centennial,*" she said. "By Michener."

"I know. I don't think you noticed me until you finished it, and it was at least eight hundred pages long."

"I noticed you. Right around page two hundred, I think."

He couldn't tell what she was thinking, but she looked at him with a curious expression in those hazel eyes and a knot formed in his stomach. Suddenly he knew he had to be very, very careful. He'd assumed he was immune to her—after all, they hadn't seen each other in twelve years—but the woman Anne had grown into intrigued him as much, maybe even more, than the girl he'd loved so many years ago.

She crossed her legs, unknowingly revealing another inch and a half of sleek thigh. He remembered those thighs, too. Chris gulped.

"I'll get the champagne," he managed to say, standing up and waiting for her to follow him into the aisle. He stepped back and put her in front of him, then with his hand lightly on her back guided her through the near-empty lobby to the crowded porch. Chattering voices soon surrounded them as they headed to the gazebo bar.

He'd give her a glass of champagne, make light conversation about the summer weather and the array of plants in the theater's garden, then take her home to her father and her daughter. For his own peace of mind, Chris knew he had to stay far, far away from Anne McNally.

That resolution lasted through the second act, until
he heard her laugh again and again. The sound bub-
bled out of her, and made him smile despite the fact that
he'd heard the lines a hundred times in rehearsal. Her
laugh was so contagious Chris wondered if he could
pay her to sit in the audience every night.

"Well?"

She turned to him, still applauding for the cast assembled onstage for the final bow. "They were fantastic."

"Let's hope the critics feel the same way." The applause faded and people began filling the aisles.
"Thanks for keeping me company."

"Are you always like this during a performance?"

"Only when I own the theater."

"I think I remember you worrying about the reviews
that summer."

"I sent the clippings to my mother. She kept a scrapbook, so the pressure was on. Now you'll have to start
a book for Martha."

She winced. "Don't remind me."

"Come on," he urged, standing up to take her hand.
"You can tell me all about it in the restaurant."

"You own a restaurant, too?"

"Just the building. We lease it to someone else to run,
and we have a nightly cabaret act after the show. It
won't start until *The Music Man* does, though. I should
talk to your father about auditioning for it."

"Aren't we going the wrong way?"

"I want to check on something backstage. We'll go
out the back."

They climbed the steps to the stage and went behind
the curtain to where small groups of people huddled
and laughed, giddy with relief the show was over. Ev-

eryone said hello to Chris, and looked at Anne with curious expressions. He introduced her to several people, spoke to the assistant director, then took Anne out to the back deck and down the stairs.

The lilac bush, the one where they used to meet, had tripled in size, still covering the corner and most of the side of the building that used to house the actors for the season. Large purple blossoms dangled from the branches, filling the night air with the fragrant scent of lilac.

Anne paused to touch one of the blossoms.

"You remember, too," he said, wishing he could see her face in the darkness.

"Of course," she answered, stepping away from the heavy blossoms. "Do the actors still live here?"

He let her change the subject, although he would have preferred discussing lilacs and secret embraces. "No. We own a house in town for them. Now this is where we build all of the sets."

"Where do you live?"

"I built a house next door. You can't see it from the road," he explained. "It's not quite finished yet, but it's good enough for the summer."

"What about the rest of the year?"

"I have a place in New York. We're thinking about taking *Music Man* on the road this year, so I'm not sure if I'll be in the city or not."

"The last time I saw you, you were headed off on a tour with *Chorus Line*. What happened after that?"

"You want twelve years in a nutshell?"

"Not necessarily. The long version is fine." So he walked her down the cobbled brick path to the building that housed the restaurant and lounge, and sat across from her in a private booth and ordered drinks and grilled chicken sandwiches and told her about his life for the past twelve years. He skipped the part about his marriage lasting nine months, or the reasons it failed so quickly. But he told her about the places he'd traveled to, and the parts he'd played until he'd discovered he liked the work backstage more than the work in front. A couple of commercials had given him the capital to make investments that led back to Matunuck and the Theater by the Sea.

Anne listened, asked questions, and when their plates were empty and she said, "I should be going home now," Chris realized he hadn't learned one thing about her.

And he wondered, as he scrawled his name across the check and Anne slid out of the booth and hooked her purse over her shoulder, if she'd planned it that way.

They walked past the lilac bush on the way to the gravel parking lot, and he wished he could take her in his arms and kiss her, just once to see if she was really Anne, the girl he'd fallen in love with so many summers ago.

But he didn't, just as he didn't take hold of her hand during the first act. Despite her agreement to go out with him tonight, he'd known she hadn't accepted easily. She hesitated by the lilacs, as one weighted branch of flowers bounced in the ocean breeze and barred her way along the path. Chris didn't stop to think about what he was going to do.

"Anne," he said, as she turned her face up to look at him, ignoring the blooms brushing against her shoulder.

He bent lower and touched her lips with his, a petal-soft kiss scented with lilac and flavored with memories. His hands rose to hold her shoulders, her skin the barest brush of satin under his fingertips. Twelve years disappeared into the night breeze as if they'd never existed at all.

Her lips parted, as if by surprise, and he took advantage of the small motion. He tasted her then, touched her lips with his tongue until they parted again allowing him entrance. He pulled her closer, despite the bushy petals crushed near his arm, and kissed her as he remembered kissing her. Long moments later, when he lifted his lips from hers, Anne looked away and stepped back.

"I'm not going to apologize," he said, trying to hide how shaken he was. What on earth did he think he was doing?

"There's no reason to," she whispered, then cleared her throat and added in a normal voice, "I really should be getting home."

"My car is over there," he said, pointing to his dark-gray sedan. He didn't dare take her arm, or risk touching her again. He stepped back and let her precede him down an incline and across the gravel lot, but managed to open the passenger door for her.

She lived half a mile down Card's Pond Road, the narrow road that paralleled the Atlantic coast. On the left were fields, a few houses and more fields full of hay or the beginnings of the sweet-corn crop. They passed the road to Carpenters Beach, where a colony of tiny summer houses lay. And then, on the left before the road ended at Matunuck Beach Road and the Matunuck grocery store, Anne pointed out a small white ranch house.

Chris pulled into the driveway, but before he could park the car she hopped out. "Thank you for a lovely evening," she said, her voice low.

He had absolutely no idea if she meant it or not.

"I'm glad you enjoyed it. You'll be at the theater a lot this summer, you know, with your father and Martha." *And with me.*

She didn't agree with him, but instead said goodnight and shut the door. He watched her walk up the path and, under the glow of the porch light, open the front door and go inside the dark house.

Chris backed the car out of the driveway and drove slowly back to the theater. He hadn't expected to feel this way again, hadn't planned to fall in love with Annie McNally twice in one lifetime. But now that he had found her, he wasn't about to lose her once more.

SHE WOULD WORK in her garden, she told herself. Invite her neighbor over for iced tea. Read the new Susan Isaacs novel she'd just taken out of the library. She would not think about last night, kissing Christopher Bogart by the lilac bush. She would not think about how warm his lips were and how exquisitely familiar his hands felt on her shoulders, or how his tongue—

"Mom! Someone's at the door for you!"

Damn. Anne hurried out of the kitchen and through the living room, where Martha stood with the door wide open. A young man stood framed in the doorway, his arms full of purple lilacs.

"Mrs. Winston?"

Anne closed her mouth, realizing it was hanging open like a dry-docked fish.

"Yeah, that's her," Martha informed the bearer of the flowers. "Someone sent her flowers?"

The young man nodded.

"Who?" Martha asked, looking back at her mother and then to the flowers.

"He said she'd know," he said, gulping. He looked past Martha to Anne, who walked to the door and took the bouquet of flowers. "You do know, don't you?"

"Yes." Anne inhaled the scent of the lilacs, holding them gently. She looked back at the young man and smiled. "Thank you for bringing them. They're beautiful."

"Oh, you're welcome. I'm glad you like them. I'll tell Chris."

Martha let the screen door bang shut as the boy went down the walk and to a beat-up Buick. "*Chris?* You mean Mr. Bogart?"

"Yes." Anne turned and went into the kitchen. Martha followed her.

"*He* sent you flowers?"

"Obviously he did." She owned only one vase, a large crystal antique she'd found in a shop in Wakefield. If it didn't hold all the flowers she'd have to put them in drinking glasses.

"But why?"

"He knows I like lilacs."

Martha scooted around until she cornered her mother at the sink. "Grandpa said you knew Chris a long time ago."

"That's right."

"Did you go out with him a long time ago?"

Anne hesitated. "Yes."

Her daughter grinned. "And now you're going out with him again. Pretty neat, Mom."

"I'm not 'going out' with him."

"Why not? I think he's pretty... cool."

High praise, Anne noted. "I'm not really interested in going out with anyone right now."

"That's what you always say."

"Well, it's true."

"Did my birth father live in Rhode Island?"

Anne stopped arranging the lilac blooms and turned to look down at her daughter. "What brought that up?"

Martha shrugged. "I thought I could meet him. If he lived here."

"You've never said anything like that before."

"I think having a father would be . . . neat." She bit her lower lip.

Anne dropped the flowers and bent down to hug her daughter. "I'm sorry, honey. I didn't know you missed John that much." Her husband had been a workaholic, hardly ever home. He played seemingly endless rounds of golf on the weekends, therefore successfully avoiding any kind of family time together. Toward the end, Anne had wondered if the man even knew what being part of a family meant.

"Jenny asked me where my father was, and I didn't know what to say. I told her my *real* father lived in Rhode Island, but she said I was lying, because if he really lived in Rhode Island he'd come over and see me and take me places and mow the lawn. Jenny's father mows the lawn and has a big garden and coaches the softball team."

All the things fathers were supposed to do, according to an eleven-year-old. Anne put her hands on Martha's shoulders and knew she couldn't lie to the child, but it wasn't time to tell the truth, either. "I've been thinking about getting in touch with your birth father, too."

Martha's eyes grew round. "You have? Really?" Then she frowned. "I thought you said you didn't know where he was."

"I think there are ways to find out, honey. But it's a grown-up decision, and something I have to take care of myself. If it's what's best for you, then I'll do it. But you'll have to trust me on this one, Marty."

Martha looked at her mother for a long minute. "Okay, I guess," she agreed finally. "Do you think he'll want to meet me?"

Anne nodded. "Yes," she said, hoping it was true. "I know he will."

Satisfied, Martha left the kitchen in search of her grandfather. Anne inhaled the sweet smell of the fresh flowers and wondered if she'd done the right thing. Martha wanted to meet her father, but Chris didn't even know he had a daughter. Would he want one? Or was the past best left alone, its secrets undisturbed?

"Do you want me to take the car and drive us in, or do you want to drop us off?"

Neither, she wanted to tell her father. *I want you to stay home and go to the beach like everyone else in South County.* "I'll drop you off," she managed to say. "I need groceries anyway."

"I'll call you when we're done," Dan promised. "Since this is the first rehearsal, I don't know how long they'll go each day."

Martha finished her cereal and took her empty bowl to the sink. "I hope everyone's nice."

Her grandfather answered. "Why wouldn't they be?"

Martha glanced over at her mother. "What's wrong, Mom?"

"Nothing." Anne gave her a quick, reassuring smile and took another sip of her coffee. She hadn't been awake very long, which was the least of her problems. A few more cups of caffeine and she'd be able to handle Martha's show-business career. She'd spent the past ten days obsessing over the end of school, Martha's show-business career, her own job interviews and, most of all, telling Chris that Martha was his. If only Martha hadn't seen the article in the newspaper...life would certainly be simpler. She could have spent the summer like a normal woman and just worried about money. Instead she'd read newspaper reviews of *The Odd Couple* and listened to the soundtrack of *The Music Man* at least eight hundred times.

"Drink up, Mom. We have to be there at ten."

"That's forty-five minutes from now. I think we'll make it."

Dan refilled his coffee cup. "Don't you want to put some makeup on?"

Anne turned to her father. "What are you talking about?"

He shrugged. "You never know who you'll run into."

"We're in the middle of a heat wave," she said. "It's going to be in the nineties today." She looked down at her white shorts and light blue T-shirt. "I think I look fine."

"You do," Martha said. "Just don't forget to put lipstick on."

"I'm thirty-one," Anne reminded her. "You're eleven. Quit ordering me around."

Dan grinned. "Touchy this morning?"

Touchy? Of course not. She hadn't heard from Chris since he'd sent the lilacs. You'd think he'd fallen into the Atlantic and disappeared. Not that she thought he'd call, but there was always that possibility. He'd sent the lilacs as a gesture of friendship, nothing more. She told herself the heart-stopping kiss had only stopped one heart: hers. And it wasn't going to happen again. Not if she could help it. "Maybe I'm nervous for both of you."

"I'm not nervous," Martha protested. "Kinda excited, maybe. I just won't know anyone there. Do you think it'll take long to make friends?"

"You already know three people: Chris, Becky and me," her grandfather assured her. "By the time the show opens we'll be like one big family." He turned to Anne and winked. "Right, honey?"

"Right." She stood up and put her empty cup in the sink. "I'll go get that lipstick on." By the time she'd slid behind the wheel of her six-year-old Ford, she'd put on a glossy bronze lipstick and brushed her dark-blond hair until it shone. She had no intention of running into Chris this morning, so naturally he was at the curb when she drove the car alongside the old white warehouse on Woodruff Avenue.

Handsome as ever in oatmeal shorts and a black polo shirt, he had stood with his hands in his pockets, as if he intended to stand there forever. Or at least until his Amaryllis arrived. He took his hands out of his pockets and shook hands with Dan when he stepped out of the front seat onto the sidewalk.

Martha was only a few seconds behind him. "Hi, Chris. We're not late, are we? Mom never drives over the speed limit."

"You're right on time," he assured her. "Are you ready to be an actress?"

"Yep. Grandpa's gonna help me."

"You have a good teacher." Then he bent down so that he could look into the open window to Anne. "Hi."

"Hi." Thank goodness she'd put Golden Bronze on her lips. With luck she'd look a couple of years younger.

"Would you like to come inside and see the rehearsal hall?"

"Well…" She wanted to watch Martha, all right, but she didn't want to spend any more time with Chris than she had to. It wasn't good for her conscience, or her heart.

"You're welcome to see some of the rehearsal, make sure Martha is being treated okay." The twinkle in his eyes let her know he was teasing.

"Please, Mom?"

Feeling like an idiot, Anne turned off the car's engine. The plan to avoid Chris Bogart obviously wasn't working. "All right. Is it okay if I park here?"

"Sure." He walked around the car, opened her door and waited for her to step onto the pavement.

"I thought stage mothers were barred from rehearsals."

"I'll break my own rules this morning."

"I guess that's an advantage to being the boss."

He walked beside her on the sidewalk. "Did you like the flowers?"

"Didn't you get my message?"

"Yes, but I wanted to hear it from you."

"I liked the flowers," she assured him. "I would have told you in person, but you weren't at the theater when I called."

"I've been in New York," he explained, following Martha and Dan to the door of the building. "Last-minute casting problems."

Martha and Dan continued on to the stage, where a large group of people gathered, unaware that Chris stopped to murmur close to Anne's ear. "Did you think, Annie, that I would just let you go?"

"Yes," she said, ignoring the frissons of pleasure his breath sent against her skin. "We just can't pick up where we left off twelve years ago."

"Why not?"

"We're older and wiser," she whispered, hoping no one would notice they'd stopped. "It's a cliché, but it's true."

"I'm a hell of a lot smarter than I was then," he countered. "And I'm not so old that I've forgotten the scent of lilacs or the way we felt about each other."

"Chris—"

"Have dinner with me tonight."

"For old times' sake," he urged. "We'll stay away from the lilacs and talk about the weather."

She had to smile. "That's tempting."

"Quite a heat wave we're having. You wouldn't believe how bad it was in the city."

"Really?"

"See how easy this is? We could manage dinner together. I did all the talking last time. Now it's your turn to tell me about you."

Anne took a deep breath. He'd handed her the perfect opportunity. Maybe a civilized dinner would be the best time to say, "By the way, remember the girl you hired for the play? Well, she comes by her talent naturally."

"Well? What do you say? You have twelve years to tell me about, you know."

She looked up into his dark brown eyes and felt her courage dissolve like sugar in hot tea. He hadn't changed much, just grown better looking. The little lines at the corners of his eyes gave him character. She'd always liked character in a man. Too bad she hadn't married it.

John was safe, business oriented and predictable. He'd also been cold, aloof and dull. The divorce had been a relief, like opening a new box of crayons after having only one brown crayon for years.

Chris Bogart was a one-hundred-and-twenty-eight-crayon box.

"Tonight would be fine," she heard herself say.

4

"HI, MARTHA. I'm sorry I'm late." Chris entered the living room as Martha held open the door.

"That's okay," the child said. "Mom's not ready anyway."

"She's not?"

"Nope. Major problems with wardrobe," she confided. "How'd I do today?"

Chris would have given a lot to know what Martha considered to be "major problems," but the little girl's big hazel eyes looked up at him with such a serious expression he knew he had to answer her question. "You did fine. In fact, you were very professional."

"Really?"

"Really." She looked exactly like her mother, especially with that skeptical expression on her face. "I'm the producer and the director, so I should know, right?"

She grinned. "Right."

"Would you tell your mother I'm here?"

"I think she knows."

He glanced at his watch. "Want to tell her again?"

"Well, okay."

Martha hurried out of the room and Chris had a chance to look around. The living room was small, but bright and neat. Bookshelves lined the opposite wall, and a television perched on a chest in the corner. A braided rug covered a large portion of the hardwood floor. Next to an overstuffed couch, framed photographs filled one wall, and Chris stepped closer to examine them. Pictures of Dan and Edie in different costumes mingled with those of a chubby baby he assumed was Martha. Martha in various poses as a growing toddler, then a little girl, and finally, one of Anne and Martha wrapped in towels, sitting on the beach. He peered closer, trying to figure out what beach.

"Dad took that one last winter when we were visiting him in Florida," Anne said, coming into the room.

Chris straightened and turned to the woman walking toward him. She wore a short white skirt and a blue silky tank top that fluttered past her hips and revealed tan shoulders. Her dark-blond hair shimmered to her shoulders, revealing a glimpse of gold hoop earrings. "No major problems that I can see," he murmured, looking at her.

"What?"

"Martha said there were 'major problems,' which was why you didn't mind that I was so late."

She smiled. "Just the usual predinner date-with-an-old-boyfriend anxiety attack."

He would never understand women. Or believe them. Anne appeared as calm and cool as if she had never given their dinner together one anxious thought. "I'm not sure if I should be flattered or appalled."

Anne's lips turned up. "Appalled will do just fine."

"That's easy enough," he replied. "It's part of being a director."

"Would the appalled director like a drink?"

"Yes, but let's go out and have one."

"All right. I'll tell Martha we're leaving."

"Is there a baby-sitter?"

"No, but Dad's home, so she won't be alone. He's in the shower, or he would have come out to say hello to you." She left the room for a moment, returned with a white jacket over her arm and a matching purse. "All set," she said.

He opened the front door and let her out. "I'm sorry I'm so late. It wasn't as easy as I thought it would be to leave tonight. I tried to call, but the line was busy."

"Martha was on the phone. She phoned her best friend in California to tell her all about the rehearsal and her song in the show. I think she sang it for her five times."

He held the door open and watched Anne's legs as she slid onto the front seat. "She did well today."

"Really?"

"Martha asked that, too. Yes," he said, pausing before he shut the car door. "*Really.*"

By the time he walked around the car and slid behind the steering wheel, Anne had adjusted her skirt and wondered why she'd worn something so, well, Californian. It wasn't a miniskirt, or even close to being immodest, but its hem landed a couple of inches above her knee. She should have put the long sundress back on. Or the green sheath, except she'd worn that the last time. It was just too hot to wear anything with sleeves, especially since few restaurants in southern Rhode Island worried about air-conditioning. And she'd wanted to look good, especially when she told Chris that he was a father.

She didn't know how looking her best would help, but she wanted to look good. She'd thought it out carefully, rehearsed the words, anticipated every reaction he could possibly have. Now all she needed was the nerve to say the words.

"I made dinner reservations in Newport," he said. "I don't spend as much time there as I'd like to."

"I've only driven over the bridges a couple of times since we moved here," she admitted. "I keep promising myself a day to tour the mansions and walk along the wharves."

"So you don't mind?"

"Of course not."

They headed toward Route 1, then to the road that took them over the bridges that connected Rhode Island's mainland to the islands of Jamestown and Portsmouth, and into the town of Newport. Popular since colonial times, the harbor town was a favorite of tourists worldwide. Yachts and sailboats competed for space in the small harbor, and lavish mansions lined the waterfront on three sides of the island. Traffic heading off the island was heavy, but Chris had little trouble negotiating his car along the waterfront to narrow Thames Street. The summer season was in full swing, even for a Tuesday night, when Chris parked the car in the area reserved for Christie's customers.

He smiled sheepishly as he stepped out of the car. "I've heard about this place. It's supposed to be where 'everybody' goes for dinner."

"I've heard of it, too," she said, opening her door and looking toward the two-story white shingled restaurant facing the water. A large covered deck sat off to one side of the second floor, and white tables were scattered on the patio near the parking area. "I'm impressed."

"Good," he declared, walking to her and taking her hand. "I wanted to impress you, especially since I don't remember ever being able to afford to take you out for a real dinner when we younger."

"I don't remember minding." *I remember walks by the ocean and holding hands in the balcony and picnics on the beach.*

"Remember all the peanut-butter-and-jelly sandwiches we ate that summer?"

"We ate them on the beach, so no matter how I wrapped them, there was always sand in them."

"Made them taste better."

"We'd snitch sodas and apples from the kitchen and think we were going to have a feast."

"We did," he murmured, tightening his fingers around her hand. "Always."

It was the perfect opening: *peanut-butter sandwiches weren't the only thing we made that summer.* But the words stuck in her throat.

Before she knew it, they were seated on the upper deck, ordering gin and tonics. The breeze, heavy with salt, blew gently toward them off the water, and an occasional cry of a sea gull could be heard over the gentle hum of conversation at the tables around them. When they went downstairs to the dark intimacy of the dining room, Chris arranged for a table in front of a window, so they continued to watch the boats in the harbor while they waited for their waiter to appear.

It would be the perfect evening, Anne decided, if she didn't have the truth hanging over her head. The longer they talked, the more she wondered if she was making the right decision.

She'd loved Chris Bogart years ago for many reasons—his kindness, talent, sense of humor and sexy eyebrows. She liked the way he smiled and loved the way he touched her. Those things hadn't changed, except she was over thirty now and knew that there was more to a man than sexy eyebrows and sensuous, thrilling hands.

"Anne?"

She glanced up to see the wine steward standing by the table. She looked at Chris and resolved to stop drinking gin and keep her mind off sex. "Sorry. I was daydreaming."

"Would you like another drink or a glass of wine?" he asked, and the amused tone in his voice told her he'd asked the question before.

"Wine, please. A glass of Chablis."

"Just a minute," Chris told the man.

He examined the wine list briefly and ordered a bottle of something Anne thought sounded expensive.

"Very good, sir."

Chris handed him the wine list. "We'll order in a few minutes."

"I'll tell your waiter that you're in no hurry, sir," the steward said, leaving the table and making his way across the crowded dining room.

"What were you thinking about?"

She shook her head. "Nothing important."

He appeared disappointed. "You're not going to tell me."

"Of course not."

"You used to tell me everything," he said.

Not everything. "I was pretty young."

"Nineteen."

"Yes."

"You haven't changed." He leaned back in his seat, his gaze never leaving her face. "Quieter, though."

"Divorce can do that."

The wine steward returned with the wine, waited for Chris's approval, then filled their glasses.

Chris touched his glass to hers. "Here's to another summer together."

"And to the success of *The Music Man*," she added, taking a sip of the wine.

"Yes, I'll drink to that, too." He took a sip of the wine and then looked around the restaurant, a satisfied expression highlighting his face. "I've wanted to come here for a long time."

"Why haven't you?"

"I couldn't find a date."

She shook her head. "You expect me to believe that, when you spend your life working with all those beautiful actresses?"

"I don't date actresses," he stated.

"Why not?"

"Too many complications."

"Name one."

"You have to wonder if they're sleeping with you because you're the producer."

"And are they?"

"Sometimes. Enough for me to realize it's not worth it. Also, it's unprofessional."

Her eyebrows rose. "So who do you go out with?"

"Beautiful mothers of actresses."

She shouldn't have been pleased with the compliment, but she couldn't help feeling pleased by his attention. He'd certainly picked up some smooth lines in the past years. But she knew that as soon as the summer season was over, he'd be off to New York or Los Angeles or wherever the work took him, because this was a man who was ambitious and talented. Too ambitious and talented for Matunuck, Rhode Island.

"You're frowning at me," he declared. "Why? You don't like it when I call you beautiful? You are, you know."

"Thank you, but—"

"There's no 'but' about it. You're still as beautiful as you were when I met you. What happened to your marriage?"

"Now I'm going to really frown at you. Why do you want to know about that?"

"You said 'divorce does that to you.' Makes you quiet. You want to tell me about it?"

She shook her head. "I'd rather look at the menu."

"Coward."

"No kidding." She opened her menu and pretended to read it.

"You owe me your life story."

"All the seafood looks wonderful."

"I did all the talking last time."

"I love shrimp and scallops."

"How long were you married?"

"Or maybe the grilled halibut."

"Have lobster," he insisted. "I owe it to you after all that peanut butter."

She put the menu down. "You don't owe me anything."

"I think I'm going to have the lobster. And yes, I do." He picked up his menu and glanced at the pages before putting it down. A waiter immediately appeared at his elbow.

"Would you like to order now?"

"Yes?" Chris looked at Anne.

"I'll have the shrimp with the crab stuffing," she told Chris. "And a bowl of chowder."

"What dressing would you like on your salad, madam?"

"Italian."

"Very good." He picked up her menu and turned to Chris. "And you, sir?"

"Broiled lobster. Chowder. Baked potato, ranch dressing on the salad."

The waiter paused to refill their wineglasses before leaving.

Chris leaned forward. "Now, Annie, you can't avoid it any longer. You have to tell me about yourself. You finished college at U.R.I.?"

"Yes." She took another sip of her wine, appreciating the way it eased each tense muscle of her body. She didn't tell him it had taken her five years instead of four. Or why. "In education."

After the soup was served, Anne managed to keep the conversation away from herself throughout the dinner. Chris was perfectly willing to answer her questions about the theater, relate funny stories about the backstage misadventures of *The Odd Couple* performances and share New York gossip about people she'd once known when her parents had performed there. Until they ordered coffee, Chris had seemed perfectly willing to forget his curiosity and keep the conversation light.

"Now," he said, ignoring the coffee cup placed before him. "Who did you marry?"

A harmless-enough question, but obviously Chris wasn't going to give up. "John Winston."

"How did you meet him?"

"Friend of a friend of a friend. He was getting a master's degree in Boston and planning to set the financial world on fire."

"Did he?"

"His own corner of it, yes. We moved to San Diego and lived there for quite a few years."

"What happened?"

Anne took a deep breath and put her trembling hands in her lap. The time for truth had finally arrived, and she'd have to explain a lot more to Chris than why her marriage broke up. "I woke up one morning and realized I couldn't live like that any longer. That Marty and I deserved something more."

He looked at her intently. "What was missing, Annie?"

"Love." She tried to smile, but it didn't work. "There wasn't any love in that house. No matter how much I tried, nothing I did made any difference. John's life was his work, and when he wasn't working, he was playing golf. When he wasn't playing golf he was at meetings and business conferences. The last couple of years were pretty lonely, even with my teaching job."

"How long were you married?"

"Seven years."

She waited for him to do the subtraction. It didn't take him long.

He gave her a curious look. "Martha isn't your husband's child?"

"No."

"She looks just like you."

"Yes, except for the hair. And she has her grandmother's voice. I could never sing a note."

"So you came back to Rhode Island after the divorce because you always liked it here, and now the three of you live happily ever after in South County."

"That was the general plan. Until you advertised *The Music Man* auditions in the newspaper."

"One of my better ideas," he informed her. "Otherwise I would never have found you again."

"We could have run into each other someday. It's a small town."

"Not in the summer. Besides, everything I do pretty much revolves around the theater. I won't have too many more nights off until *Music Man* is onstage and running smoothly."

"I enjoyed the dinner. Thank you." She picked up her coffee cup. "What time are rehearsals tomorrow?"

"Dan will have to be there at nine, but the kids aren't rehearsing until the afternoon. At one, I think. I'll give out schedules tomorrow."

She glanced out the window. The sun had set while they finished their dinner, a pink-and-peach sky that hung over the water of the harbor for long, delicate minutes before fading into charcoal. "It's been a beautiful evening."

"She has her father's hair?"

Anne turned back to him, at his long handsome face framed with dark waving hair. "Yes."

His dark eyes burned into hers. "How old is she, Anne? Nine? Ten?" Anne couldn't speak, so he prodded, "Tell me she's ten, Annie."

"She's eleven."

"Did you meet someone that autumn, Anne? While I was in Europe and you were taking classes?"

"No. There was no one after you."

They stared at each other across the flickering candlelight in the middle of the small table, until Chris finally whispered, "Are you going to tell me about it?"

"I've wanted to tell you for days now, since I first saw you again, but I didn't know how."

"I'll help," he growled. "Is she mine?"

Anne hesitated.

"*Is she mine?*"

"Yes."

He let out a long breath, and leaned back in his chair. Then he looked out to the harbor as though trying to remember where he was. The hum of conversation and the tinkle of silverware filled the silence around them, but didn't penetrate the heavy silence between them.

Anne watched him, and would have given a year of her life to know what he was thinking as he gazed at the harbor. A long, sleek yacht slid from a nearby mooring and headed toward the sunset. Anne wished she were on it. She turned away from the window and faced Chris. "I found out I was pregnant in November, two months after you left. It must have happened the last time we were together, at the beach." She paused, wondering if he even heard what she was saying.

"Go on."

"You were gone, on that tour, and my parents were doing a show in New York—I can't remember which one. They'd rented an apartment for a while, so it must have been a good job."

"You didn't try to contact me?"

"No."

He turned to her, his dark eyes unreadable. "Why not? Didn't I deserve to know I was going to be a father?"

"You'd left, Chris. What we had was over and you'd gotten the big break you'd been waiting for. What was I supposed to say? 'I know you don't love me anymore and you're in Europe being a star, but I'm pregnant'?"

"That would have been a good start."

She shook her head. "What we had ended that first weekend in September, when the show ended and you left."

"I asked you to go with me."

"And I wanted to go to college instead of following you around the world."

"It could have worked."

"You think so? With a pregnant girlfriend?"

"I would have married you."

"I didn't want to be married because you felt you 'had' to." She reached out, hoping he'd take her hand. He reached over and clasped hers, and the warmth flowed between them, giving her comfort. "I loved you. I was very young, and—" she smiled "—ridiculously noble."

His thumb caressed her knuckles. "So, I'm a father."

"Yes."

"Didn't your husband mind raising another man's child?"

"He didn't seem to care about her one way or the other, really. He was kind to her, but they never connected. And he wasn't home much."

"Why in hell did you marry him, Annie?"

"I thought he was just what Martha and I needed. Which of course was the wrong reason to get married. I believed I was in love with him—he was steady and quiet and secure. He just couldn't love me the way I needed to be loved."

"So you packed up Martha and headed east. Did you ever think of finding me and telling me about my daughter? There were any number of ways you could have done that, you know."

"I thought it was better to leave the past alone, until Martha was old enough to ask questions. I'd promised myself I'd get in touch with you when she was older."

"Does she ask about me?"

"Sometimes."

He tightened his fingers around hers. "And what have you told her?"

"That you went away before you knew about her and that I couldn't find you to tell you."

"As if I'd deserted the two of you?" He swore and dropped her hand. "She's going to think I'm some coldhearted son of a bitch who didn't want her."

"No. Never that."

His eyes were cold as he gazed back at her. "How can you be so sure of that?"

"She told me a few days ago that she wants to find her father."

"Did you tell her he was right down the street?"

"I told her he might be in Rhode Island."

"How does this work? Tomorrow you tell her he might be in South Kingstown and the next day you tell her he might be in Matunuck, until eventually you tell her he might be the man sitting in the living room?"

"You don't have to be sarcastic. This is hard enough without—"

"*Hard enough?*" he repeated, leaning forward. "You tell me that little girl is my daughter, that she thinks I deserted her? How in hell can it get any harder? And how am I supposed to make it up to her, to both of you?"

"There's nothing to 'make up.'"

He didn't appear to have heard her. "How do we tell her?"

"We don't."

"Yes, we do. I'm not going through the rest of her life as the invisible man."

"She's not ready for this."

"I disagree."

"You don't know her."

"That's the general problem, isn't it? And not exactly my fault."

"Give me some time."

"How much?"

Anne hesitated. A couple of years would be perfect, but she didn't think Chris would agree. He didn't look as if he was in the mood to agree with much of anything. "The summer."

"The week."

"The summer."

"The week."

"Until the show is over."

"Until rehearsals end." He leaned back. "That's two weeks, plenty of time for the two of us to get to know each other. She already likes me."

"As a director, not as a father."

"Give me a chance. I deserve it. Did you think that once I knew the truth I would stay away, as if it didn't matter whether I had a child or not?"

"I don't know what I thought. I only knew I had to tell you, then deal later on with what happened."

"Well, we're dealing with it now, Anne. How do you think she'll take it?"

Martha was strong and brave, and very, very smart, but she was still only an eleven-year-old child. "I think it will be okay, eventually. But you can't expect her to deal with this *and* appear in your show at the same time. Wait until the show ends, Chris. When the pressure is off her."

He leaned back in his chair and ran one hand through his hair before nodding. "All right. But when the curtain comes down on the last show, Martha meets her father."

"HE'S BEEN WHISTLING since Sunday."

Anne agreed, but added, "He's been whistling all week long."

"Uh-uh. He's been *smiling* all week. He just started whistling Sunday."

"What happened Sunday?"

Martha thought for a minute. "He went to the show."

"That's right," her mother agreed. "Chris invited him to see *Odd Couple*."

"And a wonderful show it was," her father said, stepping around the corner of the house to grin at them.

"What made it so wonderful that you've been whistling like a lovesick robin ever since?"

Martha giggled. "You shouldn't call Grandpa that!"

Dan winked at her. "You're right, my darling." He walked across the lawn to examine the vegetable garden. "She certainly shouldn't. Looks like you'll have zucchini pretty soon."

"Now, Dad, what would you know about vegetable gardens?"

He chuckled. "Not much, although your mother would talk about settling down and planting a garden whenever she didn't get a part she wanted."

"You're changing the subject. What happened at the theater Sunday night?"

"Nothing, Annie-girl. Can't a man whistle?"

She knew when she was being railroaded. "Of course you can. Whistle all you want, Daddy."

"Chris said to say hello. He wondered why you haven't stopped in at the rehearsals."

Anne pulled off her gloves. "I didn't want to be in the way. I refuse to be one of those stage mothers, even though I'd really like to be there every minute."

Martha stared at her. "You could come if you want to. You wouldn't be in the way at all."

"Thanks for the vote of confidence, honey, but I do get a little worried about all the time you have to spend at rehearsal."

"It's okay—it's *fun*, especially when everyone goofs around and acts silly and Chris gets mad."

Anne raised her eyebrows and looked at her father. "Chris gets angry?"

"Not really. We fool around to break up the tension sometimes."

"Tension?" she echoed.

"You've forgotten?" her father asked. "You know how it gets when you throw a bunch of actors together."

"I suppose so." She stood up and brushed the dirt off her khaki shorts. "Let's not talk about the theater anymore. Let's go get ice cream."

"Not me," Dan said, patting his stomach. "I'm watching my weight. I want to be in shape for opening night."

"Which is only two weeks away," Martha reminded him. She turned to her mother. "I'll go with you."

"That's the idea," Anne said. "I've hardly seen you these past two weeks." Two weeks without seeing Chris, with her father and Martha busy rehearsing. Two very lonely weeks. No wonder her garden looked so good. She'd weeded and watered, until the plants practically glowed with good health. She'd resorted to going to the town beach by herself a few times, but even that had failed to cheer her. Sitting on a beach by herself, no matter how thick the book she'd borrowed from the local library, wasn't relaxing when her only child was rehearsing for her first stage debut with the father she didn't know she had.

"Grandpa and I have had a lot to do," Martha said. "I know all my lines, but some people keep making mistakes."

"That happens." They walked together down the paved street to Matunuck Beach Road, then turned toward the ocean and the Vanilla Bean, a sturdy building that served a multitude of ice-cream flavors and desserts.

"Chris doesn't get mad very much," Martha assured her. "He's really nice to me. He makes jokes. Stupid jokes, but that's okay."

"You still like all this show-business stuff, don't you?"

"I *love* it. Becky is so sweet and Johnny—he's the star, you know—is the best dancer I've ever seen, even better than Grandpa. All the girl dancers smile at him and try to talk to him all the time."

"I don't think I know him."

"You'll have to meet him. He can sing, too. *Not* as good as Grandpa."

"Of course not."

"And the other kids are okay. Jessie is kinda shy, but Adam is really funny. He talks a lot, and he does a really funny lisp because the boy he plays in the show has a lisp and is really embarrassed about it and that's why I—I mean *Amaryllis*—teases him because he can't say my name because there's an 's' on the end and people with lisps can't say the letter 's.'"

By the time Martha took a breath, they were stepping up to the outdoor window to order ice-cream cones.

"What flavor?"

"Tin roof. Can I have a double scoop?"

"Okay. Two double scoops," she told the teenager at the window. "One tin roof, one chocolate chip. With chocolate sprinkles."

"Goody," Martha cried.

Anne pulled the bills out of the pocket of her shorts and paid for the ice cream, then waited for the cones to appear. The girl handed them the ice cream and then gave Anne the change. With napkins wrapped securely around the sugar cones, Anne and Martha strolled back the way they'd come, along the side of the road. A small white car slowed down as it approached them, and Anne tugged on Martha's collar to move her into the grass at the side of the road. The car stopped near them and backed up. Anne looked again and saw Chris stick his head out the window and yell something.

They stopped.

"That's Chris!" Martha grinned and waved her ice-cream cone at him.

"Quit doing that," Anne said. "The ice cream will fall off the cone."

Martha gazed down at her cone and gave it a cautious lick. "It's okay," she announced. "Look, he's getting out."

"I see that." Anne had spent the past two weeks wondering if he'd ever speak to her again, yet she knew he had to: after all, they had a child in common. Surely the odd frissons of sexual awareness were only on her side.

Chris walked up to them and eyed their ice cream. "That's where I was heading."

"What flavor?" Martha asked.

"Tin roof."

"Me, too!"

Chris shot Anne a look that said "What else did you expect?" Anne glanced away. Chris hesitated. "Too bad we missed each other."

"You go get some," Martha said. "We'll wait."

"We will?"

"Sure. Can we go to the beach?"

Anne swallowed a lick of ice cream and chocolate pieces. "We're not wearing our bathing suits."

"We could walk near the water."

Anne looked over toward the beach. The town had erected a wooden walkway, with showers, bathrooms and a covered pavilion, for the town residents. She wouldn't mind a walk on the beach with her daughter, and there was no reason to hurry home.

"I'll catch up with you," Chris said.

She knew when she was outnumbered. "All right."

The entrance to the beach parking lot wasn't far away. They walked along the winding private road that led to the parking lot, then onto the wide walkway and down the stairs to the beach. The sun beat down hot and strong, but despite the heat, the beach wasn't as crowded as she'd expected.

They'd successfully avoided each other for two weeks, so why was he seeking her out now? There had to be something on his mind, and Anne was afraid he'd be only too happy to tell her.

She'd been right to stay away from him. Chris was too handsome, too sure of himself and too appealing. And she had to be strong. She'd fallen for him once, but it was not going to happen again. She and Martha were not going to have broken hearts at the end of the summer. Not if she could help it.

5

CHRIS SAW THEM as they walked along the shore, kicking through the waves as the water tickled their ankles. They made quick work of their ice cream. Chris stood on the pavilion's deck and watched them at the water's edge. He finished his single scoop of ice cream, anxious to join the two of them. One was his, the other had been his a long time ago.

His daughter. The words still sounded odd, no matter how many times he mouthed them to himself. He'd watched her at the rehearsals, watched each mannerism, tilt of her head, the inflection in her voice and the proud look in her eyes when she made it through a complicated scene without a mistake. He watched and studied and still didn't see any of himself in the child. In his daughter.

He never doubted Anne's words, though. He knew how much she'd loved him that summer, how in love they'd both been. He had never understood why she wouldn't go with him in September. It would have worked out somehow.

But he couldn't blame her for having her own plans and dreams; he'd simply been selfish, demanding that the two of them be together, under his conditions and not hers.

Well, now it was the three of them. Still not together, but that was only a matter of time.

He tossed the remainder of his uneaten cone in the trash can at the bottom of the stairs and slipped off his worn boat shoes, leaving them beside the drift fence. He stepped carefully between the blankets on the crowded beach. It looked as though everyone in town was trying to survive the heat wave this afternoon. The offshore breeze blew his hair and cooled his skin. Anne and Martha turned around when they reached the rocky construction that ended the beach, and headed back toward him. Chris walked faster to catch up with the two McNallys.

"Where's your ice cream?" Martha asked.

"I ate it already."

"What kind did you get?"

"I told you, tin roof."

"With chocolate sprinkles?"

"Not this time."

Anne shaded her eyes and looked up at him. "Taking a day off?"

"Absolutely. I think we all needed it."

"Martha was starting to get tired. Dad, too, although he wouldn't admit it."

He grimaced. "I'm sorry. I've tried to take it easy on the kids and keep the rehearsals for them down to just a few hours, but it's not easy."

"We don't mind," Martha assured him. "We play Uno when you don't need us."

He knew that. Knew everything the child did from the time she arrived at the rehearsal hall until her grandfather took her home.

"Still," Anne said, looking down at Martha, "I don't think you should get worn out."

Martha grinned. "I'm not tired! And I know all my lines."

"You probably know your grandfather's lines, too." Anne sighed.

"Yep. And most of Becky's. By the time the show starts I think I'll know everybody's," Martha announced proudly.

"I'd better watch out," Chris said, "or you'll want my job next and you'll be directing the whole show."

Martha shook her head. "No way. I like being onstage. You don't have any fun at all."

"What makes you so sure of that?"

Martha shrugged. "You don't look too happy."

"I'm not supposed to," he explained. "I'm the director. I'm supposed to be making sure the actors do a good job. I'm your first audience."

"I can't wait for opening night."

"You still have two weeks," he reminded her.

"I know." She danced around him, her tiny feet making impressions in the wet sand. "It's going to be so cool."

"I think so, too."

Martha gave him another grin and ventured farther into the water.

"Don't get too wet," Anne cautioned.

"I'll dry in the sun," she countered.

"It's up to you." Anne turned back to Chris. "That was quite a conversation."

"Our daughter never runs out of something to say, does she?"

"Shh, she might hear you."

"She's in the ocean, Anne."

"Still—"

"I've been doing a lot of thinking, Annie. Why haven't you answered my calls? I didn't want to call too often and make Martha wonder, so I had to back off."

"I didn't know what there was to say to you."

"You tell me I have a daughter and then you tell me there isn't anything to say?"

"Words aren't going to change anything."

"The word *father* has sure as hell changed my life. You don't want me around, do you?"

"That's not—"

"Yes, it's true, all right." He shoved his hands in his pockets and walked beside her as she followed Martha's progress in the surf. "I don't want to fight with you, Annie. I just want to figure out how to be a father."

"I thought you didn't want a family."

"Are you going to hold the words of a twenty-two-year-old against me forever?" He looked down at her, noting the stubborn set to her mouth. He wished he could kiss the frown from her lips, wished they were alone so he could take her in his arms and convince her she belonged with him. "I'm Martha's father. I'd like to act like it."

"You can't. I don't want her to know yet."

"Why not?"

"She's not ready for something like that. We agreed, remember?"

"She likes me," he protested.

"That doesn't mean she has to know that you and I once . . . well, that we were in love with each other and made some mistakes."

"She's not a mistake."

"She might think that. I don't want her knowing yet. She has enough on her mind with the show."

"She seems okay to me," he said, pointing to the child in the surf. She bounced knee-deep in waves with two other ponytailed girls in pink bathing suits.

"Those look like our neighbors," Anne said. "Marty's been a little shy around them. One's a year older and one's a year younger." She turned back to him. "What good will it do, Chris? After this summer, you'll be off again. It would just hurt her too much."

"I would never hurt her," he said, meaning those words from a place in his heart he didn't know existed. The thought of hurting Martha made him physically ill.

"Then be her friend, not her father."

"Does she have a bike?"

"Yes. Why?"

"Fathers teach their children how to ride bikes."

"She already knows how, Chris."

"Oh. What about swimming?"

"She's had lessons."

He grinned. "What's left?"

"Sports," Anne announced. "I'm hopeless at anything athletic, and she says she wants to play softball next year."

"That's next year," he protested. "I'm talking about now."

"I know you are. But you'll be gone after the season is over. Right now she thinks of you as a friend. She won't mind saying goodbye to a friend in the fall, but she can't lose a father. You must see that, don't you?"

A friend. His daughter could only think of him as a friend, a director, a neighbor. "No. Now that I know she's mine . . ."

Anne stopped, facing the ocean and the dancing figure knee-deep in the water. "She doesn't belong to you, Chris."

"She's my daughter."

"Biologically."

"And that gives me the right to be with her."

Anne shook her head. "Maybe it was a mistake to tell you."

"Only if you try to take it back." He made a resolution to find out what his legal rights were. If any, that is. He didn't want to wage a war with Anne over Martha, but what could he do if she tried to keep the child from him?

"I want to be fair," Anne said. "I don't want Martha to be hurt."

"I wouldn't do anything to hurt her," Chris promised. "You'll have to trust me on that, Annie. You never would have told me she was mine if you'd thought I'd do something to hurt her."

She turned to look up at him. "I'll give you the time you need with her, as long as you promise you won't tell her who you really are."

He didn't really have any choice. "All right."

Martha ran out of the surf toward them, the edge of her shorts wet from the ocean spray. "It's warmer than it was last week!"

"Come on, it's time to head home."

"I'll give you a ride," Chris offered. "I parked my car in the lot."

"It's not far to walk," Anne protested.

"It's no problem," he countered. He had no intention of ending their afternoon together so soon.

When they reached the house, Dan and a vaguely familiar older-looking woman were sitting together on the front steps. Chris turned off the engine and stepped out of the car as if he'd been invited to spend the rest of the day at the house.

"Hi, Dan. Marie."

"Marie?" Anne echoed. She got out of the car and let Martha climb out of the back seat. "Doesn't she work at the theater?"

"Grandpa's friend," Martha whispered.

Anne kept her voice low. "Grandpa's friend?"

"The whistle," the child reminded her mother.

"*Oh.*" Marie was the reason Dan walked through the house whistling a happy tune? Anne didn't blame him. Marie was lovely, with short silver hair and big brown eyes.

"Hello," she said.

"Honey, I'd like you to meet a friend of mine, Marie Jameson. She's an usher at the theater. Marie, this is my daughter, Anne Winston, and my granddaughter, Martha."

Marie reached out to shake Anne's hand. "And the local librarian."

"We met at the theater, didn't we? That's why you look familiar. And you work at the Hale Library on Route 1."

"That's right. You've been there?"

"Just a few times. It looked like a very cozy place."

"We try to keep it that way," she said. "Your father has told me so much about you."

"I brag," he admitted with a smile. He turned to Chris. "Where'd you come from?"

Martha sat on the grass, beside her grandfather's feet. "At the Vanilla Bean. We got ice cream and then took a walk on the beach."

"You didn't ruin your dinner, did you? I'm trying to talk Marie into staying and having hamburgers with us."

"Well, I—" Marie began.

But Dan interrupted her. "Don't say no again, Marie. Chris, you'll join us, won't you? I'll start the grill in about an hour, which gives us time for drinks in the backyard. I made some low-fat crab dip."

"His crab dip is legendary," Anne told Marie. She hoped she'd agree to stay. Anne certainly wanted to know more about her. She waited for Chris to refuse, saying he had something important to do on his only night off.

"That sounds good to me," he said instead, surprising her. Surely hanging out with Martha couldn't compete with whatever plans he'd made for his night off.

"It does?"

"Sure." He grinned at her. "I like hamburgers. And I remember your father's cooking."

Dan laughed. "You remember that, Chris? We used to have some good parties, didn't we?"

"I've never forgotten. The only good food we got that summer we ate at your house."

Dan turned to Marie. "The people who owned the theater back in those days didn't treat the actors as well as Chris and Dennis do now."

"We do our best," Chris agreed. "But the phrase 'starving young actor' sure fit back then."

"Well, you do a good job running a theater, Chris. *The Music Man* is a pretty big production."

"Our most ambitious yet."

"The scenery alone." Dan shook his head. "It's extraordinary."

"Wait until you see the train."

"And the front porch," Martha added. When four pairs of adult eyes stared at her, she confessed, "I saw them in the back, in the shop. They let me watch once."

"You don't have to look guilty," Chris assured her. "It's okay. The sets aren't a big secret."

Dan stood up. "Come on, then. Let's take this party to the kitchen, where it's a little cooler. Who wants a gin and tonic and who wants lemonade?"

LATER, SHORTLY AFTER sundown, Anne switched off Martha's bedside lamp and watched the child climb into bed. She kissed Martha good-night, ignored her final weak protests that it was too early to go to sleep and left her to get some rest. After all, there was rehearsal tomorrow.

Once outside in the hall, Anne hesitated, reluctant to return to the back deck and the candlelit picnic table. Her father had been telling stories about show business, making the rest of them laugh with his tales of Dustin Hoffman and Carol Channing, among others. Anne had heard the stories many times before and never tired of them, but sitting next to Chris in the summer-scented darkness brought back too many memories of her own, memories too painfully sweet to be recalled or felt again.

The best she could hope for, Anne decided, leaning against the wall and hearing the laughter from the sliding-door screen, was that the more she saw him, the more she would grow accustomed to him. He would become familiar, and therefore less intriguing.

At least, that's what she told herself. If, like the old saying, familiarity breeds contempt, at least familiarity could breed a little apathy.

Apathy would be a big improvement.

"YOU'RE READY?"

"As ready as I'll ever be," Martha replied, sounding

very much like her grandfather.

Anne took a deep breath. They still had an hour before Martha had to be at the theater, but Martha had insisted on bathing and doing her hair three hours earlier. Little Martha McNally was taking no chances on what she figured was the opening night of her show-business career.

"How about something to eat?"

"I couldn't."

"Butterflies?"

"A zillion trillion."

Dan's cheerful whistle echoed down the hall, and he stopped in the doorway of Martha's room. "How's everything with my girls?"

Anne answered, while Martha made a face. "She has a few butterflies."

"That's natural."

Martha looked hopeful. "It is?"

"Of course," her grandfather assured her. "Didn't Chris tell you? We'd be worried about you if you *weren't* nervous. Your grandmother used to throw up before every performance."

Anne knew that was an outright lie. She'd seen Edie McNally apply a final coat of nail polish, then five minutes later step out onstage, cool as you please. "What about you?"

He held out trembling hands. "See? Steady as a rock."

Martha laughed. "No, they're not, Grandpa."

"Oh, well." He shrugged. "That's part of the excitement. Once you're onstage you'll remember everything you're supposed to do without even thinking hard about it. All those weeks of rehearsal will come back to you."

"Really?"

"Really. Just take a few deep breaths backstage. I'll be right there with you, you know. We have to take care of each other."

"What if I throw up?"

He shrugged. "There's a bathroom backstage. You throw up, wash out your mouth and get ready to go out there and say your lines. The audience will never know."

Oddly enough, Martha looked comforted. "Okay."

Anne urged her toward the door. "What would you two stars like to eat?"

"Something light," Dan said. "Is there any of that turkey left? I'd love a sandwich."

"Me, too," Martha echoed, slipping her hand inside her grandfather's as they followed Anne to the kitchen. "And potato chips and pickles."

"Coming right up," Anne said, willing to fix them anything they wanted as long as they didn't talk about being sick. She prepared three sandwiches, but when the time came to chew, her mouth was too dry to swallow comfortably. The actors in the family had no such trouble, though. Anne disguised her nerves by saying she'd eaten a big lunch just a couple of hours earlier.

The show was at eight, so they had to be there at seven at the latest. Since it was only five o'clock, Anne insisted Martha lie down on her bed and rest. "You don't have to close your eyes," she told her. "You can read or listen to your radio. Just take a rest, because you've got a late night."

"Good idea," Dan said, winking at Anne. "I'm going to get into my chair and maybe I'll doze off while I'm reading the newspaper."

The hours went by slowly, despite Anne's trying to read a book Marie had recommended as a "good beach book." She had trouble keeping the characters straight, wondering if Martha would remember all the words to "Good Night, My Someone."

When it was time to go to the theater, Dan told Anne to stay put until seven-thirty. "Remember, this is just a dress rehearsal."

"With an audience."

"An audience that's given free champagne and reduced ticket prices."

"I know. But—"

"But nothing, Annie-girl. Martha will be fine. She has me."

"I don't think I can sit here alone in this house."

"Go early and keep Chris company. He'll need it."

"Now *that* I doubt."

"He has twice as much reason to be nervous about tonight." Dan lowered his voice. "He's never been a stage father before."

HE'D HAD some tense opening nights, like the time the star of the whole damn show had been too drunk to step onstage, and years ago in New Jersey, when the theater had caught on fire and burned down before the curtain could rise on act 3. But this was the worst. The biggest production they'd tried so far, with sets that cost a small fortune and weighed more than a herd of elephants. And of course, the stomach knotter of all, a daughter making her stage debut in a not-so-small part in a not-so-small production.

His only comfort was that Dan would pull her through. Chris examined the situation backstage. The assistant stage manager hurried past, a clipboard in her arms.

"Is everyone here?"

"Yes." She nodded. "They're getting dressed now. Johnny's running through his dance routines and Becky's warming up her voice. The little ones are dressed and playing cards with a couple of the dancers."

"No sign of trouble?"

"The wisteria keeps falling off the front porch."

"Get me a staple gun," Chris ordered. At least that was something he could do. He looked at his watch. Forty-five minutes until show time. They hadn't opened the doors yet and wouldn't start seating people until the stage manager gave the word.

A stagehand came with a staple gun, but didn't give it to the director-owner-father. "I'll take care of it, Chris. You don't have to worry."

In other words, get out of the way. His job was done, at least for now. Until after the show, when he'd discuss the night's performance with the cast. Until tomorrow morning, when they'd rehearse again until the snags were ironed out. His job wouldn't be over until after Friday, when the critics arrived and the reviews were written. Then he could hand things over to the assistant director and the stage manager.

"Thirty minutes," Dan announced, his booming voice hearty with anticipation.

Chris could use some of the older man's confidence right about now. "How is she?" he asked.

Dan knew exactly who he meant. "Fine. A few nerves earlier, but no different than the other two kids. They're all pretty excited, but they'll settle down."

"Good." He ran a hand through his hair and looked to see if anyone was listening. Despite the bustle of the stagehands, no one paid them any attention, except to glance toward Chris every so often. "This isn't an easy night."

"No," Dan agreed. "I can see that."

Chris shoved his hands in his pockets. "I was never this nervous before one of my own performances."

"It's not easy being a father."

"I would have married her if I'd known," he stated, meeting Dan's clear eyes. "She could have found me."

Dan cleared his throat. "I should have insisted. I owe you an apology for that one."

"I can't say I'm sorry I fell in love with your daughter, but I should have been there for her."

"She didn't let you." Dan clapped a hand on Chris's shoulder. "How could you have known?"

Chris shot him a rueful grin. "It's not easy being a father, is it?"

Dan shook his head, dropping his grip on the younger man's shoulder. "You're just getting your feet wet. Wait till Marty starts growing up."

Chris shuddered. "I don't even want to think about it."

"Are you going to be around?"

"Yes." His voice was firm, a statement no one would dare argue with. "I'm going to be around, all right."

ANNE TOOK a long shower, hoping the tepid water would cool her down and relax the tight clutch of nerves in her stomach. Stage fright wasn't limited to the actors, she realized. She wondered if there was an expression for what stage mothers experienced on opening night. Wrapped in a towel, she stood in front of her small closet for a long time, wondering what to wear. She'd worn the green dress before, for *The Odd Couple*. And she'd worn her white skirt and blue top the night she and Chris had gone to Newport for dinner. That left one dress, a swirly black knit sundress with a square-cut bodice and wide shoulder straps. She could wear black sandals and gold earrings and feel totally overdressed.

Which was the privilege of a doting stage mother, after all. And preferable to wearing the green dress again. She looked at her watch. The curtain rose in forty-five minutes, and she wanted to get there early, in case Marty needed her. She could dress in fifteen minutes, especially since her hair could be pinned up in a quick chignon for the evening. It was too hot to wear it long anyway.

By seven-thirty she'd parked in the grassy parking area across from the theater and joined the crowd crossing the road to the front porch. She didn't see Chris, so she wandered to the garden and the cupola, where champagne was being served.

"Mrs. Winston?" the young bartender asked as he handed her a plastic glass.

"Yes." She didn't recognize him.

"Chris told me to watch for you. He left a ticket for you at the box-office window. He said he'd try to catch up with you before the show started, but if he didn't, he'd meet you inside."

"Thank you." She told herself she wasn't disappointed that he wasn't waiting on the porch, as he had the other time. She wanted no romantic involvement with him, after all. He was Martha's father, and that was it.

Still, her traitorous heart skipped a beat when she saw him step out from the crowd on the porch. He wore a light-colored shirt and beige slacks. Anne hesitated, wondering if she should make her way through the crowd to the porch. He might not be looking for her; there could be a hundred other reasons why he would be standing at the front of the theater.

She moved toward him anyway.

He waited at the top step and took her hand. "I didn't recognize you at first." He looked at her hair, then his gaze ran the length of her body. "Very sophisticated, Annie."

"Inside is a quaking stage mother."

"It doesn't show," he said, drawing her close to him without dropping his grasp on her hand. "If it's any comfort, I know just how you feel."

Their gazes met, an intimate sharing of their predicament as parents to a budding actress. Anne looked away first, hoping to break the intimate contact. She couldn't do this, couldn't fall in love with him all over again. She refused to let this happen twice in one lifetime. "How is she?"

"Playing cards with the other kids backstage."

"Really?"

"According to your father."

Anne let out the breath she'd been holding. "Does she need me backstage?"

"I don't think so, but I can find out."

"I'm wondering why I ever let her get involved in this in the first place."

Chris tugged her toward the closed doors. "You'll know shortly, Anne. When she's onstage and you're bursting with pride and the audience is applauding for her. Then you'll know."

"Applause has never meant much to me," she muttered, following him inside the lobby. He picked up a headset on a corner stool and spoke into it, then lifted the receiver to his ear. "Ten minutes?" he asked.

He walked back to her. "We're going to seat late, in ten minutes. You have time for more champagne."

"And Marty?"

"Just fine. The cast has become attached to those kids, so I'm sure they're taking good care of them."

"Of course they are," Dennis agreed, coming up to stand beside them. He grinned at Anne. "I was eavesdropping." He turned to Chris. "T.J. wanted to know when he could open the doors."

"Ten minutes is the word backstage." Chris looked at his watch. "No one expects us to be on time for the dress rehearsal."

"Thank God," Dennis said. "This is going to be one hell of a production. Your father is great. Too bad we couldn't have given him a bigger part. He could probably play the music man, Professor Hill, himself."

"Oh, he has," Anne informed him. "In seven different countries."

"I'm not surprised. That man has stories—"

"Dennis!" a woman called from upstairs. "I've got a bird flying around up here!"

"Excuse me. One of the ushers needs my expertise."

Chris chuckled. "Come on," he said, taking Anne's hand again. "We'll go around the back and see what's going on."

He led her down the right aisle and past the orchestra pit, where the various musicians were warming up. Then up the stairs to the stage, then behind the curtain on the right into bedlam.

"Watch your step," he cautioned. "We don't have much room back here. The sets take up most of the space."

Anne watched as stagehands piled luggage on top of the berths of a train car. Red leather seats faced each other, and straps hung from the ceiling for the "passengers" to hold on to. "It looks so real."

"They've worked hard on that, and we only use it for the opening scene. After that it's wheeled backstage, then out onto the deck and into the other building during intermission."

Anne hadn't expected anything so elaborate. "It's incredible."

"You haven't seen anything yet."

"I don't think I want to, at least not backstage. I'd rather see it from the audience, with all the magic still in place."

"There's magic, all right." He touched her cheek. "I still think it's more than just luck that we ended up here together, this summer."

"Magic?" she echoed, trying to calm her thundering heartbeat.

"Of course," he said, caressing her cheek. "That's one of my specialties."

"Mom! What are you doing back here?" Martha ran up to them, giving Chris a curious look as he dropped his hand and stepped back to allow the tiny vision of early-1900s childhood to stand in front of her mother.

"Coming to see you. You look beautiful."

Martha frowned. "I wanted to surprise you. I didn't want you to see my costume until the show."

"That's my fault," Chris interjected. "I wanted to show your mother some of the sets, and she was just in the process of telling me that she wanted to see the show first. You didn't tell me that your mother believed in magic."

Martha shook her head. "Of course she doesn't. She's a mother."

"And mothers belong in the audience," Anne added. She gave Martha a quick kiss. "Break a leg, honey."

"That's what Grandpa said, too."

Chris took Anne's hand. "Well, he's 'the music man.' He should know."

6

"WE CAN GO upstairs to the balcony if you want," Chris offered. "If you have trouble seeing, let me know."

"This is fine." Almost every seat downstairs was filled, and Anne sat beside Chris in the last row, reserved for the staff. Several people held clipboards, and the sound board was set up nearby. The same bearded young man wearing headphones bent over the equipment, making adjustments and examining the various colored lights. Anne gazed at the rows of people in front of her, people talking and laughing and fanning themselves with the slick programs, and wanted to demand, "Be kind to my daughter! She's never acted before!"

Chris shot her an anxious look. "Are you all right? You seem a little pale."

She tried to smile. "I can't help being nervous."

"You look like you're going to jump up and run out of the theater."

"I have a good reason."

"She'll be fine. It's in her blood."

"Dan uses that expression all the time." She smoothed her dress over her lap in a nervous motion. "Just because she comes from a show-business family doesn't mean her mother isn't going to explode from secondhand stage fright."

"No one ever died from stage fright, secondhand or otherwise."

"Promise?"

"Look, you were just backstage fifteen minutes ago. You saw that she was fine."

"What about you? You're not nervous?"

"I'm hiding it."

"Well, you're hiding it very well."

"I was an actor, remember?"

The music began with a loud flourish, and a medley of the show's songs began. Dennis's voice boomed out over the quieting audience, welcoming everyone to the show and asking for patience during the first dress rehearsal.

The curtains parted, revealing a train full of salesmen. Anne leaned forward as the actors began the first song, a peppy complaint about the traveling life.

Chris turned to Anne with a grin as applause erupted at the end of the number. "Well?"

"Fantastic."

He nodded. "It worked, didn't it?"

"The audience—"

"Loved it," he declared, making a few notes on the pad in his lap. Anne turned back to watch the stage as the crowd of "townspeople" danced to the "Iowa Stubborn" song. Once again the audience applauded its approval as Johnny McMann sang his warning of trouble in River City. It was Martha's favorite, which meant she'd been singing it for the past three weeks, so Anne could have recited every word along with the lead actor, even if she hadn't heard her father perform the Harold Hill role at least sixty times twenty years ago.

The first act sped by, until Marian appeared seated next to Martha at the piano. Anne leaned forward and held her breath.

"Now, don't dawdle, Amaryllis," Marian admonished, then began to sing her instructions as Martha "played" the corresponding notes.

Martha looked a little nervous, but her fingers moved along the keyboard as rehearsed while Marian and her mother sang their argument. Martha said her lines clearly, and when Winthrop appeared, his lisp getting some sympathetic laughter from the audience, Amaryllis complained to her piano teacher.

The audience grew silent as the lights dimmed and Marian and the little girl sat in the window to look at the stars and sing the beautiful ballad "Good Night, My Someone." Martha's voice trilled out clear and true, if slightly shaky at first. Becky's clear soprano helped her along, and the two finished their song to the audience's approving applause.

Anne swallowed the lump in her throat and leaned back as the set was pushed off to one side and Martha left the stage. She started to applaud, and looked down to see her fingers enclosed within Chris's large hand.

He put his other hand over their clasped ones. "She did beautifully."

"Yes," Anne agreed, hoping she wouldn't burst into tears of pride and relief. "She certainly did."

"Don't pull your hand away," he whispered, rubbing his thumb along her knuckles. "I need the support."

"You'd never know it."

"I told you, sweetheart, I'm a *very* good actor."

"I remember."

He gave her an odd look, but she turned her attention back to the stage, her fingers still entwined in Chris's firm grip. She wondered when he had reached for her, and how she could have held his hand without realizing she was doing it. Embarrassing to be sitting in the dark theater holding hands—and even more embarrassing to be thirty-one and *still* able to feel embarrassed by the gesture. How could she feel this way after so many years? She was a mother, she was divorced, she was holding hands with the father of her child in the middle of a crowded theater.

And she didn't dare let herself enjoy it.

"DID I LOOK scared?"

"Not a bit," Anne assured Martha for the fifteenth time. "You looked beautiful up there."

"You could hear me?"

She tucked the sheet up near Martha's chin. "Clear as a bell."

Martha wrinkled her brow. "Adam was really noisy backstage. He's gonna get in trouble with Debby."

"Debby?"

"The stage manager." Martha yawned. "She had to tell him to be quiet three times."

"I'm sure he was very excited."

Martha nodded. "*Everyone* was. Even Grandpa."

"I liked when he leapt across the stage. I didn't know he could jump that high."

Martha giggled. "He was funny. Did you see Marie?"

"No, was she working up in the balcony?"

"No. She just came to see Grandpa in the show."

"Really?"

"I think she likes him, don't you?"

"I suppose she does."

"I like Chris."

Anne looked down at her and gave her a quick kiss on the forehead. "It's after midnight. You'd better get some sleep."

"Don't you like Chris?"

"Of course I do."

"You knew him a long time ago, didn't you?"

"Sure. You know that."

"He acts like he likes you a lot, Mom."

"Well . . ."

"Do you like him?"

"You're talking boyfriend-girlfriend stuff, am I right?" Martha nodded. "I thought so." Anne sighed. "I can't answer that question, Marty. It's private, and I don't have the answer anyway."

"Has he kissed you?"

"Martha Jane!" Anne exclaimed. "You've gone too far." The child giggled, making Anne join in. "You've been singing too many love songs, young lady."

SHE TOOK her coffee onto the front step and felt the faint brush of the ocean breeze along her skin in the morning sunshine. It was going to be another hot day as soon as the sun burned through the haze.

Dan and Martha would most likely sleep most of the morning, but Anne found it hard to stay in bed, even though she'd gotten in bed at the same time as the actors in the family last night. They'd been pretty excited after the show had ended, and Anne knew there would be a succession of late nights now.

Chris must be thrilled. It was clear that he and Dennis had a hit on their hands. Once the critics saw the show on Friday, it should be a sellout every night. The finale, "Seventy-six Trombones," had brought the audience to its feet in a two-curtain call ovation. Unusual for a dress rehearsal, Chris explained with pride.

Anne took another sip of her coffee and wondered when she would see Chris again. He hadn't released her hand until intermission, then had picked it up again and tucked it within his at the start of act 3. Martha's scenes had continued to go well, and Dan was his usual competent and charismatic self.

Now, if she could only get used to the late nights and late mornings and euphoria over "standing o's" . . .

Somehow she wasn't surprised when she looked up to see Chris standing at the end of her driveway.

"Good morning."

He hesitated, as if unwilling to disturb her, then moved across the lawn toward her. "I thought you'd be sleeping in."

She shook her head. "Not today. What are you doing?"

"Walking to the market for coffee and a newspaper."

Anne knew she shouldn't, but she wanted to hear his reaction to the show last night. She wanted to hear how wonderful their daughter had performed one more time. "I don't have a newspaper, but I can give you a cup of coffee."

"I'd like that."

"Come on in. Dad and Martha are still asleep."

"We won't wake them?"

She lowered her voice as she opened the screen door. "We'll go out on the deck in back."

In minutes she'd poured more coffee and led Chris out to the deck to take a seat at the picnic table. He sat down close to her and leaned back. "I didn't expect this."

"Neither did I."

"I wasn't talking about the coffee."

She glanced up at him, saw the expression on his face and set her cup carefully on the glass tabletop. "Don't, Chris."

"Why not?"

"None of this makes sense."

He frowned. "Why should it? Seeing you again, after all these years, wasn't something I expected. And finding out about Martha, being a father to an eleven-year-old, wasn't something I'd anticipated either."

"I know. Maybe I shouldn't have said anything after all."

"I'm glad you told me. More than glad," he added. "But how can you expect this to make sense? If I told you I'd never stopped loving you, would *that* make sense?"

"No," she answered, her voice soft. "It wouldn't."

"You're not making this easy, Annie."

"Neither are you."

"I've tried," he admitted, his dark eyes crinkling at the corners. "You have to admit that. You're not going along with the program."

"Which is?"

"To fall into my arms."

She couldn't help smiling. "I did that enough times when I was younger."

"I got used to it. Could you do it some more?"

She'd like nothing better than to fall into those very strong, very capable arms and give in to every passionate thought she'd had about him, but the common sense of an older, wiser woman prevailed. She stood up, hoping he'd take the hint. "I don't think that would be a good idea."

He didn't look at all convinced. "We'll see. I have the rest of the summer to convince you."

Which was exactly the problem, Anne knew. They just had the summer, and she was a little old for a summer romance complete with bittersweet goodbyes come September. "Would you like some more coffee?"

"No, thanks." He put his mug on the table. "I'll leave a couple of tickets—front-row seats—for Friday's performance for you. Bring a date. I'll behave myself and not act jealous and surly."

"Thank you, but I'll only need one ticket."

"Good. The cast party is after the show. Would you like to join us?"

"I'd like that, yes."

"It's going to be lonesome for you with Dan and Martha at work every night. Are you working this summer?"

"No. I've been on two more job interviews, though."

"What will you do if you don't get a teaching job?"

"Substitute until I do."

"Come down to the theater and usher."

"What?"

"The pay isn't much, but at least you'd be near Martha. In case she needed you," he added, as if as an afterthought.

"I've never ushered before."

"Marie can show you." He leaned forward. "Say yes, Annie." He reached out and took her hand. "Don't stay home all by yourself while we're having fun down the street."

She looked down at their joined hands and thought of last night. How good it was to feel another person's warmth, a man's rough skin against her fingers. "You're determined to get me into show business."

"I'm determined to get you into my life."

"I'm already in your life. You have my daughter."

"But I want more." He grinned. "Haven't you heard anything I've said? Say yes, Annie."

"I'll think about it."

"Don't think," he urged. "Just say yes."

"I think that's how I got into trouble twelve years ago." She smiled at him anyway, loving the way his voice deepened whenever he wanted his own way.

He stood up, keeping a grip on her hand. "Do it for Martha. She'd like knowing you were there."

"You're playing dirty."

"I'll play any way I can." His fingers caressed her and he pulled her toward him. His breath feathered against her lips as he bent over her. "I'm running out of time."

His lips touched hers, demanding, warm, persistent. It was heaven kissing him in the heated morning air, with summer sunshine breaking through the haze and warming her face. Heaven when he released her hand and put both hands on her waist to hold her to him.

Her lips parted, as naturally as the feelings that swept over her, as easily as standing in the sunshine in a man's embrace. She leaned into him, feeling her breasts brush against his chest, wondering if her legs would support her if he happened to let go. His tongue took her mouth, played with her tongue, danced erotically between her lips, sending frissons of pleasure and need through her. It had been so long since anyone had held her, desired her.

She remembered the way he tasted and the way his body felt against hers, inside hers, around hers. And realized that if the embrace continued, as his palms slid underneath her T-shirt and cupped her breasts, that she would be making love with him if she didn't stop it.

She didn't want to stop it, though. That was the problem. She wanted to go on kissing him until the sky cleared and the neighborhood sea gulls squawked their hunger from the field across the street.

He lifted his mouth from hers, barely touching her lips, dropping his hands along her skin to her waist, caressing her softly.

"You always felt so good in my arms." He dropped another kiss on her lips before moving away. "If we were alone . . ."

"Don't say it," she begged, her cheeks reddening.

"What's wrong with remembering?"

She looked up into his craggy, handsome face. "Nothing," she admitted, hoping he wouldn't feel her tremble under his hands. "But we shouldn't get carried away."

His eyebrows rose. "We shouldn't?"

"Don't tease."

"I'm not teasing." He tightened his fingers around her waist. "Say yes to the usher job, Annie."

She knew she shouldn't agree to something that would only throw them together for the next four weeks, but the temptation to be at the theater with Martha was too much. This way she could keep an eye on her daughter, even if it meant steeling her heart against Chris's charms. "Kind of like 'If you can't beat 'em, join 'em'?"

"What do you have against show business?"

"Let's just say it wasn't the most stable life-style for a child."

"What about for a woman?"

An interesting question, but one she'd rather not answer. "All right," she said slowly. "You have yourself a new usher."

His smile widened. "Good. You can start Saturday night. I'll meet you at the lilac bush at four o'clock."

"I don't think so," she said, reluctantly pulling back
from the compelling embrace.

"All right, in the lobby, then. We'll have dinner be
tween shows."

"We will?"

"Of course. You and I and Dan and Martha. One big
happy family."

She wished he hadn't phrased it that way.

FRIDAY NIGHT'S SHOW brought the crowd to its feet, just
as Dan said the Wednesday and Thursday shows had
The critics congratulated Chris as they filed up the aisle
to the lobby.

"Glad you enjoyed it," Chris said, shaking hand
with the critic from one of the Providence papers. *If you
write one harsh word about my daughter's perfor
mance I'll jam that pencil down your skinny throat and
ban you from my theater for the rest of your life.*

"Fantastic," the man said, moving toward the door
"You have a hit, Chris."

"It's the best thing you've done so far," a young
woman commented, slipping a notebook in her purse
"I think I'll go over to the Seahorse Bar and have a
drink."

She ventured an inquiring smile, but Chris didn'
take her up on the subtle invitation. After all, he had
an important date with his daughter and her mother.

"Thanks for coming," he said instead, flashing her
his most professional smile. Anne hadn't entered the
lobby yet, but he waited for her to appear in his line o
vision.

The young woman looked disappointed and moved
past him toward the open doors, where the crowd

poured down the steps and across the street to the parking lot.

"Chris?"

He turned to see a tall slender brunette standing to his right. "Stacey." He bent to kiss the cheek she offered. "How have you been?"

"I had a good winter," she drawled. "What about you?"

"The same."

"I thought you'd call when you were settled in for the summer."

"Well," he began, seeing Anne brush past the red curtain to the lobby. "I've been busy."

She arched her well-groomed eyebrows. "I see," she said, following the line of his gaze. She turned back to him, a knowing expression on her face. "Your latest, I presume?"

"I wouldn't put it that way."

She laid a light hand on his arm. "It was nice seeing you again. I loved the show."

"Thank you, Stace." She hated to be called Stace, and he remembered too late.

"See you around, darling."

Chris looked over toward Anne, who had slowed her steps and turned to study the pictures on the wide bulletin board. Dan and Martha had had black-and-white photographs taken last week, and their eight-by-ten glossies looked as professional as the rest of the pictures hanging on the wall. He never could have imagined he'd see a picture of his daughter in his own theater. He thought he'd marry again one day, but he'd almost given up on having children. He didn't meet many maternally minded women.

Anne wore a short white skirt again, this time with a silky black top and gold jewelry. She looked beautiful, with her sleek dark blond hair falling to her shoulders. He swallowed hard. He didn't want to mess this up, not when it had taken him twelve years to find her again.

He would like nothing better than to hurry to the lilac bush, kiss her until she could no longer protest, then walk the overgrown path to the beach and make love to her in the sheltered privacy of the dunes.

It wouldn't be the first time.

"Anne," he said, approaching her. "She was wonderful again. A real trooper."

"She was, wasn't she? There was no music on the piano. My heart was in my throat."

"They pretended beautifully, though, didn't they?"

She nodded, her eyes twinkling. "Yes. She's as good as her grandmother in that respect."

He took her arm. "Would your mother have liked seeing Martha onstage?"

"I think so. She thought the world of her, but they didn't have much time to spend together. We were in San Diego and of course my parents were all over the world. They stopped in whenever they could, though, and Martha adored both of them."

"That's obvious she loves her grandfather."

"They're two of a kind, aren't they? It used to bother me, but now I realize that they can't help being alike. And they have so much fun together. She's been good for my father."

"Here comes someone else I think has been good for your father," Chris said, nodding at the woman stepping carefully down the narrow steps to the balcony.

"They're just friends."

"Are they?"

"Of course. Marie," Anne called, swallowing the sudden lump in her throat. Lord, how she missed her mother! It was unfair to lose her so soon before she was at least one hundred and ten years old, able to see her granddaughter grow up.

"Hi again! Are you going over to the party?"

"Yes."

"Great. I hear you're going to be working with me tomorrow night. Don't worry, it's easy and most of the people are very nice."

"Thanks."

"We're going backstage," Chris said, as the last of the audience trickled through the door.

"See you in a few minutes." Marie reached for the heavy doors and swung them shut as Chris and Anne went down the empty aisle toward the stage. It didn't take long to round up Martha and walk to the restaurant along the walkway lined with an assortment of blooming flowers. Past the lilac bush, Chris noted as Anne brushed past the fading blossoms. He put his hand on Martha's shoulder as they walked to the restaurant.

"You're doing a great job, kid," he told her.

She looked up at him and smiled, her mother's eyes flashing at him. "I like it. It's fun."

"Remember, you promised to let me know if you have any problems."

She giggled. "I don't have any problems!"

The members of the cast were exuberant, happily downing punch from the large glass bowl on the bar. In the restaurant area, platters of sandwich meat, baskets of rolls, trays of sliced fresh vegetables arranged around bowls of dip covered several tables along the side of the room. A large cake, decorated with a dancing "music man," took up another table.

"Wow," Martha breathed, eyeing the cake.

"Have a sandwich first."

"Okay. I'm *really* hungry, Mom."

Chris chuckled. "Help yourself to whatever you want, honey."

Anne looked over Martha's head to meet Chris's gaze. "You're going to spoil her."

"I haven't even started yet," he whispered, as Martha moved away toward the center table. Becky handed her a plate and moved aside to let the child get closer to the food.

"Everyone has been so nice," Anne murmured.

"It's a good group," Chris agreed. "And a good show. Are you hungry?"

"A little."

He attempted to walk with her to the table of food, but was interrupted by different members of the cast and the crew who wanted to talk about this show and the next one, already in rehearsal. He lost Anne, saw her join Martha at the buffet and tried to get to them. Finally he managed to reach them as they held their plates. He pointed out an empty table and promised to join them as soon as he could. Anne waved to her father, and he and Marie headed in their direction.

Chris hurried to get a drink at the bar, brought Anne a glass of white wine to the table and sat down, pleased she'd saved a place beside her.

"Aren't you going to eat?"

"In a moment."

"He wants to bask in the glory of directing and producing a hit show," Dan explained. He turned to the younger man. "Am I right?"

"That's part of it, sure." He put an arm around Martha. "I'm proud of my young star, too."

"I'm sure you are," Dan agreed. "You have every reason to be, too."

Chris looked back at Anne, who appeared uncomfortable with his praise of their daughter. *You're going too far*, her eyes flashed. He ignored the warning. He would wine and dine her, convince her that she would have fun being part of his life, at least for the summer. After that, of course, he couldn't promise anything. Anne knew better than anyone what a life in show business meant. You went where the work was. New York, Los Angeles or East Peoria, it didn't make any difference. You packed your suitcase and followed your dream. And, he smiled to himself, you knew you were having more fun than anyone else in the world.

AFTER A LATE BREAKFAST Martha rushed off to play with Nancy and Lisa, the girls next door. Martha had finally swallowed her initial shyness and accepted their invitation to shoot baskets in their paved driveway.

"Chris is sure proud of that child," Dan commented, refilling his coffee cup. "You did the right thing, Annie-girl."

"You think so? I see the look on his face when he watches her and I think that everyone can see that she must be his."

"I don't think anyone thinks that, least of all Martha."

"I hope not, Daddy. I don't want her to be hurt."

"She'll have to know someday, won't she?" He sat down across from her at the kitchen table.

"Not quite yet," Anne declared. "There've been too many new things in her life in a short period of time. I promised Chris I'd tell her when the show was over, but I wished I hadn't made such a promise. She doesn't need a new father, too, along with everything else."

"But what about you, Annie? What do you need?"

Anne thought of Chris, his strong arms and the feel of his warm mouth against hers. "I don't think I need anything," she fibbed. "Besides, I'm not the one with the romance brewing around here, am I?"

Dan grinned. "You're talking about me?"

"You and a certain librarian."

"Marie's a nice lady."

"You're spending a lot of time with her?"

"As much as she'll let me." His smile darkened. "Do you mind, sweetheart? It's been good to have company, good to feel alive again."

Alive. Yes, Dan McNally was very much alive. "It's okay, Dad. Enjoy your summer. You deserve it."

"So do you, Annie." He stood up and dumped the remainder of his coffee in the sink, then put his empty cup in the dishwasher. "It's time for change, darlin'. Time to get on with our lives."

"That's what I've been trying to do since I left John," Anne replied. "Get on with my life."

Sympathy colored his voice. "Then it's time for the next step. Chris looks at you as if he never wants you out of his sight. He's talked you into working nights at the theater, hasn't he?"

"Yes, but—"

"He's doing what he can to keep you close, Annie. Can't you see that? The man is falling in love with you, I think. Or maybe he never stopped being in love."

"Even if he was, Dad, that doesn't change anything. He'll still be gone at the end of the summer. I don't think I could say goodbye to him twice."

"He's not twenty-one, not some hungry young actor chasing his dream, Annie. What makes you think he'd leave?"

"The nature of the beast, Dad. I know Chris. He's not the kind of man who makes promises."

And she wanted security, a home, a place to settle down in until she was ninety-two, with flowers in the garden and coffee in a pot, not in a Styrofoam cup from the nearest deli in between shows.

7

"YOU HAVE TO back off." Anne shifted her chair to the left and watched Martha move to the bar for a refill on her cola. She'd agreed to join Chris in between shows, but she was beginning to wish she hadn't.

"Why?"

"People will start to wonder."

"Wonder about what?"

"You. Me. Martha."

"No one gives us a second thought."

"Two of the dancers frowned at me tonight. And then there was that woman in the lobby last night, the one with the long red fingernails on your arm."

"So?"

"So? I'm sure you have a very active, uh, social life until now, and—"

"Had."

"What?"

"*Had* an active social life." He grinned. "Still do, actually, whenever I can talk you into going out with me. And I never date any of the dancers."

"Why not?"

"They're too young. I leave them all to Dennis, who usually gets involved with at least three of them during the season." He waved the waitress over and ordered a refill on their glasses of iced coffee. "I've never dated one of the ushers before, either. What did you think of your first time on the job?"

"It wasn't too hard, except for the four people who showed up on the wrong night."

"Did you have any empty seats to give them?"

"No. Dennis bought them a drink, and they said they'd return tomorrow. They calmed down."

"Good. Speaking of my social life, come to cabaret with me tonight. It's the opening, and should be interesting. People have been rehearsing all week, but it's still pretty spontaneous."

"Who performs?"

"Any one of the cast or crew who has auditioned. I'm not in charge of it—that's the musical director's job this year. You never know who's going to hop onstage in front of the fireplace and sing a song. I'm surprised Dan hasn't auditioned."

"He hasn't mentioned it to me, but if he jumps up and grabs the microphone I won't be shocked."

Chris laughed. "Neither will I. By the way, he's a real asset to the show. Everyone loves him backstage. They hang on every word of his stories, just like I used to. And still do, actually."

"He should write them down."

"When he retires?"

"I don't think he'll ever retire." Anne chuckled. "The last time lasted about a year and a half."

Martha returned to the table and slid into her chair. "What lasted a year and a half?"

"Grandpa giving up show business."

Martha rolled her eyes. "I don't know how *anyone* could give up show business! It's so exciting!"

And that, Anne knew, was exactly the reason she should stay away from Christopher Bogart. He wasn't the kind of man who would want to give up the exciting life he had to settle down in Rhode Island with a very unexciting schoolteacher.

If another summer affair was what she wanted, then she could have it. Trouble was, every time he touched her she forgot all of her resolutions.

"No MIDNIGHT BEDTIME tonight, young lady."

"It's my night off. Can't I have any fun?" Martha complained.

"Until nine o'clock you can have all the fun you want." Dan had taken Marie out to a late movie and dinner on their night off, and Anne didn't expect him home until after midnight. She'd planned a quiet evening home alone with her daughter, the kind they used to have before *The Music Man*. At least one night a week, Anne resolved, should be normal. Microwave popcorn, television, renting a movie or simply sitting in the front yard, eating ice cream. Anything that didn't have to do with the theater down the street.

"What movie?"

"*Sleepless in Seattle*."

"Oh, good. I love that one."

"I know," Anne said, flicking on another light. Although it was barely sunset, the sky had darkened with ugly black clouds. "Did you leave the beach towels outside on the deck?"

"Yup."

"Go bring them in. I think we're going to get a storm."

Martha brightened. "Goody!"

When had her daughter started saying "goody"? Anne hated storms, but Martha had never been bothered by thunder and lightning and had even seemed to enjoy it. "You'll have to hold my hand."

"Don't worry, Mom. I'll keep your mind off it. We can play Uno or something."

"All right," she agreed, unconvinced that a round of Uno would be any comfort. She wandered around the living room, looking out each window toward the ocean. "I'm going to put the movie on," she called when she heard the kitchen door slam shut.

"Where should I leave these?"

"Throw them on a chair in the kitchen for now," Anne said, slipping the movie cartridge into the VCR. Tom Hanks and Meg Ryan's love story would do a better job at keeping her mind off the storm than a game of cards with a child who would screech "goody" at every good hand.

"Can I make microwave popcorn?"

"Sure." She pushed the stop button and got up to help Martha in the kitchen. Soon they'd assembled everything they needed for their evening: popcorn, cold cans of diet cola and a large bag of M&M's. Anne took over her father's recliner, while Martha curled up on pillows on the floor, her bowl of popcorn on her lap.

"Can I have a dog?"

"Why a dog?"

"It would be someone to play with," Martha said as the movie began.

"What about the girls next door?"

Silence.

"They seem nice. You could invite them over here anytime you want to."

"Maybe," Martha conceded, and flicked the volume button on the remote. "I'll think about it."

Halfway through the movie the power went out, plunging the house into silent darkness. Thunder crashed outside, and a sharp flash of lightning lit the sky.

"Damn," Anne muttered. "I should have had candles ready. Do you know where the flashlight is?"

Martha giggled.

"What's so funny?"

"You *never* know where the flashlight is."

"Because you always take it," Anne answered, unperturbed. She didn't see any problem with staying where she was until the power was restored. It had happened before, and hadn't stayed off for more than five minutes. "Never mind," she assured Martha. "We'll be back to normal soon."

After a few minutes Martha moved to the couch and a better view out the window. "I don't know, Mom. It looks like a big one."

"Don't tell me that."

"You want me to lie?"

"Absolutely."

"Someone's here." Car lights briefly flared across the window.

"Grandpa?"

"I don't think so."

Anne scrambled out of the recliner. "Lock the door."

A car door slammed shut. "It's Chris!"

"Chris? Why would he be here?" She glanced down at her wrinkled cotton nightgown. Not exactly meant for entertaining, it had a neckline that plunged to a deep V between her breasts. She hoped she didn't have chocolate stains on the blue fabric. "Is my hair a mess?"

"I can't see," Martha said, going to the door.

"Good."

"Hi, Chris! Our electricity went off," the child stated unnecessarily.

"Mine, too," he said, stepping into the living room. "I came to see if you were all right."

"We're fine," Anne said, hesitating before walking closer. He shone the flashlight on the floor and stepped over Martha's nest of pillows and blankets. "We were having a pajama party," she explained.

"Want some popcorn?"

"Sure," he said, sitting on the couch. "I brought a flashlight and some candles, just in case you needed extra. I know how you hate storms," he added, his voice low.

"I guess some things don't change," she said, backing up to the chair.

"That's what I'm counting on," he answered. She could make out his smile despite the darkness. "Do you want to light these candles? It's pretty dark in here."

"I have to find the candlesticks."

"Here." He thrust the flashlight in her hand.

"We couldn't find ours," Martha explained, sitting next to him on the couch as another flash of lightning lit the sky and thunder boomed in the distance. "Mom said the power would come back on in a few minutes."

"I'll keep you company until it does."

Anne made her way to the kitchen and found the pair of candlesticks on the top shelf of the cabinets, along with the champagne glasses she never used. Maybe she ought to think about entertaining once in a while, she decided, feeling the layer of dust on the heavy silver candlesticks as she set them on the counter. She carried them into the living room, hoping Chris had brought matches. She wouldn't have any idea where her father kept the ones for lighting the barbecue.

She told herself the storm had thrown her off, and as the rain began pelting down from the sky, she refused to admit that Chris's appearance had anything to do with her frazzled nerves.

She was happy to see him. She longed to go into his arms and have him hold her. She wanted to feel his skin against hers, his mouth joined with hers, and anything else joined together, too, she thought wryly. It had been a very long time since she'd been with a man, her husband being her only other lover.

So, of course, she wished he'd go away. She didn't need a lover in her life, didn't need to love someone, didn't need to risk her heart for one more summer.

She took a deep breath and returned to the living room. Martha sat beside Chris, and in the dim, shadowed light she could see a resemblance in the way they held their heads, in the smiles they shot her as they turned from the window and looked at her.

"Chris likes storms, too," Martha announced.

"I know," Anne said, before she caught herself.

"Oh, that's right. You guys knew each other a long time ago. How long ago?"

"Years and years," Anne answered, keeping her voice light. She didn't need for Martha to find out who her father was, especially not now. And not this way.

"Before I was born?"

"Long before," Chris said, pulling candles out of his jacket pocket. "These aren't very fancy, but they should help."

"Did you by any chance bring matches?"

He rummaged through the other pocket and produced a matchbook. "Compliments of the Sea Horse lounge."

"Thanks." Anne fiddled with the candles until Chris reached out and took the candles from her. With easy motions, he steadied the candles and then lit them. The light glowed around the pine coffee table, illuminating Chris's strong features and dark-eyed gaze. Anne gulped. It was so nice to have someone take care of things.

The rain pounded on the roof, while the wind threw the raindrops hard against the living-room windows. The only good thing was the lightning had stopped, although in the distance skinny flashes of light still lit the sky to the north.

Martha leaned back on the couch. "Now what?"

"We could tell ghost stories," Chris suggested.

Anne shook her head. "No, thanks. It's too close to bedtime."

Chris turned to her, a wicked twinkle in his eyes. "What's appropriate for bedtime, then?"

She ignored his grin. "Something calm and quiet."

"Okay," he agreed, picking up one of the candlesticks. "You play, we'll sing."

"But I'm not—"

"Sure you are. How about a medley of show tunes?"

Anne knew when she was beaten. When singers started singing, there would be no stopping them. She picked up the flashlight and switched it on. "I'll go get my robe on."

When she returned Chris and Martha were huddled around the piano, going through songbooks and sheet music. The candles were grouped together, shining their light on the papers. Anne slid next to them on the piano bench and let her fingers ripple over the keys. "I'll just play chords," she said. "You can sing the melodies."

Identical grins lit their faces, making Anne glance from one to the other and hope that Martha never stood beside her father and looked in the mirror.

"Anything but *The Music Man*," Martha told her mother, shoving the pile of sheet music toward her.

Chris picked up the top paper and set it on the music holder. "How about something from *South Pacific*?"

Anne peered at the title in large print. "'Some Enchanted Evening'?"

"Seems to fit tonight."

Anne shot him a questioning look. "Enchanted? That's an odd way to look at a power outage."

"You don't call candlelight and music enchanting? I thought you were more romantic, Annie."

Martha looked at both of them and frowned. "I don't know that song."

"I do." Chris gestured toward the piano keys. "Go ahead and give me the opening notes, Anne."

She played a few experimental chords, then paused with her hands poised above the keys. "Ready?"

"Ready." Chris sang the romantic song, never taking his gaze from Anne's face. When the last notes faded, Anne looked up at him. "I guess you haven't lost your voice."

He shrugged. "I still sing in the shower."

"Can we do 'Doe a Deer' next?" Martha asked. "I love that one."

"Sure," Anne agreed. "It's easy."

They sang for over an hour, until Anne begged for mercy, Martha yawned three times in a row and Chris requested something to drink. Anne tucked Martha into bed, left the flashlight with her in case she needed to get up in the night and returned to the candlelit kitchen to see Chris pulling the cork from a bottle of wine.

"Wine? Where did you get that?"

"I brought it."

"Why?"

"I hoped to find you home. I was going to rescue you from the storm."

"The storm's over."

"Not really. There's still no electricity." He handed her a glass of white wine. "And you look like you could use this."

"Thank you. I hate thunderstorms."

"I remember." He touched his glass to hers. "To sunshine."

"To sunshine."

"And love," he added.

She hesitated before touching her glass to his. "Love?"

"A four-letter word, Annie. We've been singing about it for the past hour."

She didn't want to talk about love. "The singing was a great idea, by the way."

He took a sip of wine and leaned against the counter. His face was shadowed, out of the direct light of the candle. "I thought you might need me."

"I did," she admitted. "Your being here really helped me. And Martha."

"I would do anything for the two of you. You must know that."

"But I'm not asking for anything."

He set his glass on the counter. "I am."

Which was exactly what she was afraid of. "What?"

"How am I doing at this fatherhood business?"

The question threw her. "I don't know. Are you spoiling her?"

"I'm trying not to, although the urge to buy a pony comes over me daily."

"Promise me, Chris. No ponies."

He smiled. "No promises."

"Chris—"

"I'm teasing." His smile faded. "But I want to be a good father. I didn't know I would ever feel this way."

"You're doing fine." And she meant it. He'd come tonight, when he'd thought they'd need him. "You're here, aren't you?"

"That's not enough."

"That's a lot."

"But what does she *need*?"

Anne thought for a moment. Dance lessons. School clothes. Maybe braces. "Nothing," she replied. "I don't want your money, or child support, or anything like that. Can't you understand that I just felt you needed to know?"

"You thought you'd tell me and I wouldn't *do* anything?"

"Yes."

"That's impossible, Anne. I should be doing fatherly things."

"You can teach her how to drive a car."

"I don't want to wait that long."

"I'll give it some thought, okay?"

"Okay. Now that we have that squared away, come here."

"Why?"

He opened his arms. "Because you've looked too serious all evening, and because I want to hold you."

She stepped forward, out of the candlelight and into the shadowy darkness of Chris's embrace. His chest was hard and warm, the arms that encircled her tender and yet full of strength.

"Put your arms around me," he said, rubbing her back in up-and-down motions.

She sighed, doing as he instructed, and leaned into him. She knew it shouldn't feel so good, so safe, so absolutely right in every way. She knew she should step away, leave the warm circle of his arms and not tempt herself again. She had him only for the summer, and summers were short.

She knew how badly her heart would ache when he left, and she couldn't stand that kind of pain again.

He wouldn't release her. Instead he bent his head and looked down, forcing her to look up at him. "Remember the storm?" he whispered.

His lips moved across her forehead and lower, down to her ear and across her cheek. His breath was warm and tingling against her skin, an achingly familiar embrace.

"Yes." She would never be able to forget.

"You were alone in the loft."

"Painting sets." She laughed softly, remembering. "I wasn't much of an artist. They must have been desperate."

"I'd been looking for you. Rehearsals broke up early. No one knew where you were."

"Thank goodness no one found us." Partially naked, under a heavy paint-spattered tarp, they'd made love while the rain had pounded on the pointed roof and thunder had sounded all around them.

"We were very young, taking chances like that." His lips found hers, brushing them gently until he felt her quiver in response.

"I can't take chances anymore," she murmured against his mouth.

"Can you make love?" He kissed the corner of her mouth.

"Can or will?" She wished she didn't shiver when he did that.

"Will."

"Can't."

"I don't believe you," he said, taking her lips with a startling passion. She didn't believe it either, not after the way her legs weakened and her hands tightened around his back, or her lips opened to allow him entry. She kissed him back, as if twelve years had never happened, as if the two of them were the only people in the world, which after all was the way they'd felt that summer. And to her amazement was the way she felt right now, tonight.

His hands slid between them and parted the front of her robe, the cotton belt giving way without protest. He smoothed his hands around her waist, then higher, to touch each breast with startling tenderness.

"But Martha—"

"Can't see us in the dark," he finished for her, slipping the loose sleeves off her shoulders. He planted a kiss on her neck before urging the fabric lower, revealing the top of one breast. "I've never seen you in a nightgown before. I like it."

"I wasn't expecting company," she whispered.

"Good. I'd hate to think there was another man in your life." He smiled down at her in the darkness as he caressed her bare upper arms.

"Another man?"

"Someone other than me."

There's never been anyone else but you. The unspoken words were all too true, Anne realized. Not even her husband had touched her heart the way this man had. And continued to do.

But what did this mean to him? Another summer romance? Reliving the past? Anne slid her hands up to his shoulders, as if to push him away. "What are we doing, Chris? Reliving old times?"

His eyes darkened. "Is there something wrong with that?"

"Oh, yes." She didn't want to relive the past, no matter how tempting it would be to drop her nightgown to the floor, to make love to him the way she wanted to. Again. She'd come to Rhode Island to build a new life. Plant a garden and give Martha a home filled with peace and love. She hadn't come to repeat the mistakes of the past, no matter how tempting.

"You want to make love to me."

"Maybe," she managed to reply. "But I don't think it would be a very smart thing to do."

He shook his head. "We could—"

Whatever he was going to say was interrupted by the bright lights filling the kitchen. The refrigerator hummed loudly, and the television blasted static. The clock on the coffeemaker blinked 12:00, over and over.

"Well, I guess you don't need me anymore," he murmured, dropping his hands from her arms to lift the cotton sleeves over her shoulders. He adjusted her robe, even going as far as tying the belt in a loose knot at her waist. "Good as new," he stated, looking down at her.

"Thanks for coming over."

"Now it's your turn."

"My turn for what?"

"To come to my house." He took her hand and walked through the dining area to the living room. "Come for dinner tomorrow night. We'll eat early, so Martha will have plenty of time to get ready for the show."

"I'm ushering tomorrow night."

"See? It works out perfectly."

"I didn't know you could cook."

He shrugged. "There's a lot to catch up on, isn't there?"

He kissed her, a deep, lingering kiss that threatened to make her forget her objections to making love. When he finally lifted his mouth from hers, Anne could barely catch her breath.

"See you at five."

Anne watched him leave, then shut the door and locked it. She turned off the television and the VCR, no longer interested in the ending of *Sleepless In Seattle*. She'd seen it many times before anyway. She went to the window and looked toward the ocean. The moonlight sparkled on the tiny strip of water visible from her living room. How could she still be in love with him? It made no sense, and yet it explained everything. Why she'd settled for a loveless marriage, why she'd moved back to Matunuck. And why her heart beat faster every time Chris Bogart looked her way.

Anne touched her lips, still warm from Chris's kiss. Guess it was obvious that some things never changed.

"'THE COMBINATION of singing, dancing and fine acting make an exciting evening of theater in Matunuck,'" Dan read from the *Providence Journal*. "'A show not to be missed!'"

Anne looked up from her cookbook. She'd planned applesauce muffins for breakfast. "Do they mention Martha?"

"Not by name. 'Charming cast of children' is the phrase." He peered closer. "It's a long article." He read silently, then grinned. "Here I am! 'Dan McNally returns to the stage. Proving there's no substitute for age and experience, he lights up the stage as the constable.'"

"Congratulations." She watched as he jumped up from the kitchen table, danced around the kitchen and gave her a quick hug.

"The old man's still got it," he stated with satisfaction.

Anne laughed. "You sure do."

"Got what, Grandpa?" Martha trudged in to the kitchen.

"A good review."

Her face lit up. "Did we knock 'em dead?"

"We sure did, honey pie. You're a star."

"Let me see."

Dan folded the newspaper and pointed to the columns. "Right there."

Martha's lips moved, reading silently. Then she looked up at her mother. "I'm 'charming.'"

Anne nodded, not letting go of her wooden spoon. "I always knew that."

Martha turned back to her grandfather. "Think Chris will be happy?"

"I sure do. Right here in this paragraph they talk about the 'fine direction.'"

"That's Chris?"

"Yes. A fine director. Never saw the man lose his temper twice in one day." He handed Martha his mug. "Would my charming granddaughter pour her grandfather a cup of coffee?"

"Sure. I'll even sing while I do it." Anne moved out

of the way so Martha could reach the coffeepot. "I learned some new songs last night."

"I heard the power went out around here."

"Yeah." She put the coffee on the table. "Chris came over so Mom wasn't scared."

"Oh, really?" Her father grinned. "Nice of him."

"We sang songs, and Mom played the piano."

Dan glanced at his daughter and winked. "Oh, she did, did she?"

"Yep."

Anne felt she had to defend herself. "It *was* nice of him. He brought candles and an extra flashlight."

"Candles," her father repeated. "You sang songs by candlelight."

"Yes." Anne scooped mounds of batter into the greased muffin tins. "Is there something funny about that?"

"No, course not." He cleared his throat. "It just seems that you're doing more this summer than weeding zucchini and baking bread, that's all."

Anne had to smile. "What am I going to do with you?"

"Feed me," he suggested.

"Speaking of feeding you, I won't be doing it tonight. Chris has invited Martha and me to his house for dinner before the show."

"Well, well."

Martha put down the newspaper and grinned at her mother. "Goody!"

Anne shoved the muffins into the oven and shut the door before turning to her daughter. "You like that idea?"

"Of course! He has a dance floor in his basement."

"He does?"

"And he said he'd teach me how to tap." When Anne didn't reply immediately, Martha added, "Isn't that neat, Mom? Don't you think that's really nice of him?"

"Oh, sure," Anne was forced to answer. "Really nice."

8

THE HOUSE needed love. As Anne walked up the driveway it was pretty obvious that the man who lived there didn't have the time to make a house a home. Though it could be a very pleasant home, Anne conceded, noting the gray shingled siding and the oversize windows trimmed in white. There were no curtains on the windows or flowers in the yard. There wasn't even a yard. The house sprawled across the level ground, a flash of blue sea in the distance, with waving beach grass for lawn and a couple of pine trees that appeared to have been plopped down by mistake and stayed for twenty years.

Chris appeared at the door and held the screen door open as she and Martha walked up the stairs and across the wide deck toward the man with the smile on his movie-star face.

"I hope you like steak," Chris said. "Come on in. We'll have drinks on the deck in back. Hi, honey," he said, gazing down at Martha. "Did you see the review in the *Journal?*"

"Yep," Martha answered, looking as though she'd love to hug him. Anne watched her struggle to resist throwing her arms around him. "I'm one of the charming children."

"You certainly are," her father agreed, beaming down at her.

He seemed to want to swoop her into his arms, but he managed to contain himself and settled for tweaking one of her braids. Martha grinned up at him.

Anne watched the exchange, realizing the two of them really cared about each other. Two of a kind. No. Martha was hers, these few weeks of show business only a brief experience. Definitely not the first step of a lifetime career. Somehow she'd have to make Chris understand that.

Anne shifted the grocery bag she held by its folded top. "I brought you something from my garden."

He was surprised, and reached for the bag. "Thanks." He gestured to the kitchen. "Come on in."

They followed him into the square kitchen, a compact bright room whose windows faced the deck and Card's Pond Road.

He opened the bag. "Do I have to put these in the refrigerator?"

"It wouldn't hurt."

He pulled out the three tomatoes and two dark zucchini. "Thanks, Annie."

She suddenly felt ridiculous. Why would he care about a gift of fresh vegetables? "You're welcome."

"I just turned the grill on. Let me show you the rest of the house."

Martha glanced around the beige-and-white kitchen. "This sure is clean."

"I'm not here very much," he admitted, looking around the kitchen as if seeing it for the first time. "I haven't had time to decorate yet."

"How long have you lived here?"

"I built it a couple of years ago. This is my second summer here."

He pointed to the dining area across the entry hall and then led them into the wide living room that faced south, toward the Atlantic Ocean. It was a beautiful room, with shining pine floors and a wall of windows that faced another deck and framed the view of the Atlantic. An Oriental rug covered a portion of the floor, and an overstuffed tan sofa faced the windows, a brass lamp standing beside it. Several framed Broadway-show posters hung from the white walls, but otherwise there was nothing personal in the oversize room. "I haven't had a chance to decorate," he repeated. "I guess it looks pretty bare."

"You have a beautiful view."

Martha eyed the shining floor. "You could roller-skate in here."

He chuckled. "I never thought of that. I guess it does look a little like a roller-skating rink."

"Where's the place that you dance?"

"Downstairs. I'll get to that later." He pointed toward the hall on the left. "My study and a bathroom are that way." He headed in the opposite direction, to another hallway. "Two bedrooms and a bathroom," he explained.

Anne poked her head into his room, unashamedly curious about this part of his house. A king-size bed faced the French doors that led to the same deck the living room shared. And the same view—a wide stretch of beach grass and the greenish blue ocean in the distance. A thick beige bedspread covered the bed, but otherwise the room was devoid of color. Washed-pine shelves were empty, except for a small white lamp.

"The house certainly has . . . possibilities," Anne managed to say.

"I like the location," he admitted. "Next to the theater. An easy fifteen-minute drive to the train station. One of these days I'll have time to unpack my things and settle in."

"Do you have an apartment in New York?"

"Sort of. I've sublet half of it to a friend of mine. He's out on the West Coast now, so when I'm in New York I have the place to myself. Neither one of us lives there full-time."

He showed them the private bathroom and a smaller bedroom before leading them back to the living room.

"What's down there?" Martha indicated the other hallway.

"My study. Or at least it will be when I get around to buying a desk," he added.

No surprise there, Anne thought. Her house might be small, but at least there was furniture and pictures and curtains. "Can I do anything to help with dinner?"

"Let me get you something to drink. White wine okay, or would you like something stronger?"

"Wine is fine."

"I bought root beer for Martha," he said, disappearing into the kitchen.

Martha opened the French doors and stepped onto the deck. "Mom!"

"What?"

"Come here."

Anne followed her daughter onto the wide deck that ran along the length of the house. Two padded loungers occupied a shaded corner near the smoking barbecue grill. "What?"

Martha pointed to the yard. "There's a big hole out there."

"I'm putting in a pool," Chris said, coming up behind them. He handed Anne a glass of wine, then gave Martha a tall icy glass of root beer.

"Wow! When will it be done?"

"Soon." She went over to the edge of the deck.

"I thought she'd like that," he whispered to Anne. "Girls like pools, don't they?"

"You're doing this for Martha?"

He shrugged. "I thought she could have parties here if she wanted."

"But you live within walking distance of the ocean."

"She said once that she had a pool in San Diego."

"Yes, but—"

"I wanted her to have one here, too." He smiled. "Don't be upset with me, Annie. I didn't want her to miss her life in California."

"I don't think there's much chance of that now," Anne assured him. "But that has nothing to do with this."

"You think she's happy?"

"I think she's having a wonderful summer and starting to feel good about herself. And she's not so lonely."

He let out a long sigh. "Good."

"Tell me about the dance floor you're supposed to have. Don't tell me you added that for Martha, too."

He shook his head. "No. It's in the basement. I still tap to keep in shape, plus there's an exercise area."

"Did you tell her you'd teach her how to tap dance?"

"You don't want me to?"

"I don't want her to become one of those kids who can't think of anything but her 'career.'"

"I promise you that won't happen," he replied. "Now, how do you like your steak cooked? I can't guarantee anything. I bought the grill after eating at your house last week."

Anne shook her head. She should have known that if Chris Bogart wanted to be domestic, to play the role of caring father, he would go at it with a vengeance. With a pool, a barbecue and anything else he thought fit the part. "Medium, with a little pink in the middle."

"CAN I STEAL HER away, Marie?"

"Of course," Marie whispered, dropping the curtain that separated the lobby from the audience. "We've seated the latecomers and everyone is settled, at least until intermission. Anne is all yours."

Anne put down her stack of programs and gave Chris a curious look. "What do you want?"

"I owe you dessert." He took her hand and led her out of the lobby and onto the silent porch.

"After that big dinner, I don't—"

"Just this once don't argue with me," he urged, holding her hand tighter in his large one.

"Where are we going?"

"My house." He tugged her down the steps, away from the audience's approving applause of "Rock Island Line" and into the quiet darkness.

"But we'll miss the show," Anne protested.

"One time won't hurt," he said, leading her along Card's Pond Road until they reached his driveway. He'd left the outside lights on to illuminate the stairs to the deck.

She told herself she shouldn't be so happy to be alone with him. After all, last time they'd ended up kissing in the kitchen when the electricity was out. And kissing Chris was something that should be avoided if she wanted to keep her heart safe and insulated. Trouble was, the rest of her traitorous body remembered how wonderful making love to Chris had been. Something like that wasn't easy to forget, even though she'd tried.

"I know most of the lines by heart," Anne admitted.

"I'll remember that in case I need an understudy."

Anne laughed. "You wouldn't say that if you'd ever heard me sing."

He unlocked the door and ushered her inside, then switched on the light to the kitchen. "Come to think of it, I don't recall ever hearing you sing."

"You don't know how lucky you are."

He turned to smile down at her before planting a quick kiss on her lips. "Oh, yes, I do." Then he straightened and opened the refrigerator. "Chocolate cake and champagne," he announced. "How does that sound?"

"Decadent."

"Good. I plan to be a bad influence." He opened a lower cabinet door and pulled out a large picnic basket.

"What are you doing?"

"Fixing dessert."

"You don't do this often, do you?"

"Not really." He opened the lid, checked to see that the basket contained two glasses and tucked the bottle of champagne inside the fabric-lined basket. "Why?"

She pointed to the handle. "The price tag is still on it."

He shook his head and reached for a tightly wrapped plate Anne assumed held pieces of cake. "I was trying to impress you."

"You have," she assured him. "I've never been on a picnic at night before."

He turned to her with a wicked grin. "Yes, you have."

The memory returned instantly, and she didn't stop to censor her words. "You call that a picnic?"

"We brought sandwiches," he informed her. "After all, I was starving after the show."

She backed up a step, suddenly feeling uncomfortably warm. Sandwiches weren't part of her more vivid memories. "We're going to the beach?"

"Yep." He closed the lid and picked up the handle. "It's just a short walk from here. Just let me get a blanket and we can go."

A blanket. Champagne. The beach at night.

Seduction.

So, Anne wondered, following Chris through the dark living room and out the front deck toward the ocean, why wasn't she protesting?

Enjoy, a little voice whispered from somewhere deep inside.

No problem, Anne agreed, taking the hand Chris offered to guide her down the narrow dirt sandy path between the high beach grass. *Unfortunately, it was no problem at all.*

It didn't take long to reach the ocean. The quiet strip of sandy beach was deserted, a glow from the moon the only light and the soft patter of the low-tide surf the only sound. They stopped in a private circle protected by the dunes, still holding hands as they looked out to the water.

"Where did twelve years go, Annie?"

"I don't know. Spent growing up, I guess."

"We thought we were pretty grown up then."

"We weren't."

"I know." He brought her hand to his lips. "But, God, how I loved you."

Loved. Past tense. Why did pain encircle her heart at the word? His lips warmed her fingertips for one brief moment, until he gently released her hand and began to unfold the blanket.

"This is new," Anne said, as she reached for one corner to help him spread it out on the sand. "We don't have to—"

"It's okay. I bought it to use on the beach this summer."

Anne hesitated. It didn't seem right to use a brand-new blanket, yet she had no choice but to settle her side of the soft fleece on the sand as Chris anchored the corners of the blanket with a couple of rocks.

"There. All set." He looked up at her. "Aren't you going to sit down?"

Anne sat, glad she'd worn khaki shorts and a coral T-shirt, unofficial uniform of the theater's ushers and parking-lot attendants. If she were draped in a gauzy white dress she'd resemble something in a television commercial for mouthwash. Champagne, moonlight and a handsome man on the beach just seemed a little too perfect. She kicked off her sandals and placed them carefully on the corner of the blanket while Chris removed his loafers and tossed them aside. Then he took the champagne bottle from the basket and popped the cork.

"I feel like I'm in a movie."

He looked around, satisfaction evident in his expression. "It's just as I remembered."

Anne hugged her knees to her chest and gazed out over the water. She took a deep breath, inhaling the scent of the ocean.

"I love this beach. Martha and I take lots of walks down here." She leaned back as Chris handed her a glass, then watched as he filled it with the sparkling liquid. "You've gone to a lot of trouble. What's going on?"

He filled his own glass and touched it to hers in a silent toast. "I don't get to see you alone."

"You went to a lot of trouble for a private conversation."

His dark eyes grew serious. "I thought this might start making up for the peanut-butter sandwiches."

"You don't have to make up for anything."

He shook his head. "Yes, I do. Eleven years of Martha's life. Twelve years without you. I don't know how I can ever make it up to you."

"You don't have to. It's not as if I told you I was pregnant and you turned your back on me." She held out her glass and touched it to his. "Here's to the future, with no regrets."

He smiled, a bit rueful, as his glass touched hers. "I have plenty of regrets."

"Everyone does. That doesn't mean you should suffer from them for the rest of your life."

He didn't look convinced. "My biggest regret is letting you go."

"You didn't. We wanted different things, and I went my own way."

"With a child. *My* child."

Anne took a sip of champagne, enjoying the tickle of the bubbles against her throat. She wished he didn't care so much. It would make it so much easier not to love him. "I don't want you doing things like this because you feel guilty."

Chris smiled, setting his half-empty glass in the sand next to the blanket. He took out the platter and folded back the aluminum foil to reveal squares of dark chocolate frosting. "Oh, believe me, sweetheart, that's not it."

"It's not?"

"Not entirely, no. I'd be doing my best to be with you no matter whose mother you were or weren't." He set the plate between them. "We'll have to use our fingers. I forgot the forks."

"I'm not very hungry."

"Neither am I." He took the champagne glass from her hand and set it beside his in the sand. Then he faced her, taking both her hands in his. "Last night you accused me of wanting to relive the past."

"You admitted it."

"I was wrong."

A man admitting he was wrong? That called for more champagne. "Can I have my glass back?"

"In a second. Whatever we had twelve years ago was between two very young people. It's different now, except for the fact that I want you as badly as I did then. Common sense tells me I should leave you alone, but I can't do that. I want to be part of your life, Annie."

"You already are," she whispered. "Don't you know that?"

He leaned forward, brushing his lips against hers. "No, I don't, sweetheart. You keep pushing me away."

"I don't want to," she admitted, loving how his lips tickled her cheek as he kissed his way to her ear and lower, down the tingling column of her neck. "It's just—" She stopped. How could she tell him she still loved him? And she never wanted him to know?

"Just what?" He leaned back to look into her eyes. She shook her head, and disappointment clouded his gaze. "I thought you were finally going to be honest with me. Every time I get too close you pull away."

"It's best that way."

"If that's the way you want it, then there isn't anything else I can do." He turned away, refilled her glass and handed it to her. "Should we talk about the weather?"

She sipped the champagne, wondering why she felt so sad now that she'd gotten what she said she'd wanted. She tilted her head back toward the dark sky. "Beautiful moon tonight."

"Yes. Almost full."

She tucked an errant strand of hair behind her ear. "Wonderful breeze."

"Think we'll get rain?" He turned to her and began to laugh. "I can't sit here and talk about the weather, when all I want to do is make love to you."

"We need rain," she whispered. "There's a tropical storm off the coast of Florida, so—"

"Come here," he commanded softly, opening his arms.

Anne didn't hesitate. She placed her glass in the sand and leaned toward Chris's wide chest. His arms encircled her, making her feel that she was the only woman in the world who mattered to him.

Even if that was just a mirage, she wanted to believe it, at least for a while. Pretend that he was hers, for "always," like the words to a song her father used to sing to her so many years ago. Her arms went around his neck as his mouth claimed hers in a surprising, fierce motion that took her breath, and all her objections, away. Still on her knees, she rose to meet his embrace. His mouth slanted against hers, her lips parted to deepen the kiss. He tasted the way she'd remembered, and the warm male scent of him filled her senses.

Twelve years dropped away as the shimmering moon folded them in its magical light. She was nineteen again, with the man she was in love with, when making love was brand-new and every touch was an intriguing experience.

Anne felt the breeze whisper against her bare skin as Chris tugged the T-shirt up her back. They broke the kiss only long enough for Anne to tug the shirt over her head and toss it aside. She reached for Chris, to tug at the buttons of his white shirt. He helped her, their fingers tangling in button holes and crisp cotton fabric, until he shrugged the material off his shoulders and onto the blanket.

He touched her smooth shoulders, edging the straps of her bra down her bare arms. "I remember this part," he said, smiling into her eyes.

"It's all coming back to me, too."

"We were always in a hurry," he mused, his fingers tickling the lace at her breasts and lower, unfastening the clasp and tossing the fabric aside.

"We were always afraid we'd get caught," she reminded him, shivering with pleasure as his hands cupped her breasts.

"You were always so beautiful, and just a bit shy."

"And you were patient." He'd been so careful with her, hesitant to hurt her or embarrass her. He'd let her decide how far to go and when to stop. And when she hadn't wanted to stop, one dark night, he'd made certain the pain was short-lived and the pleasures intense. Just the memory threatened to take her breath away.

"I don't feel patient now," he whispered, thumbing the sensitive nubs of her breasts.

"Neither do I." Twelve years was a long time to dream of one particular man. She didn't want to wait one moment more.

She went into his arms, her breasts brushing erotically against the soft crinkly hair of his chest. Skin to skin, mouth to mouth, they tumbled down onto the soft blanket. He slid his hand beneath the waistband of her shorts; she tugged at the zipper of his slacks. They rolled to their sides, kicked off the rest of their clothing and came together in a naked tangle of heated skin. He urged her onto her back and she reached to pull him to her, but he stopped for a moment, moving away in the darkness.

When he came back to her, he moved his entire body on top of hers, covering her with his skin, pushing her thighs apart with one knee.

"Thank you," she murmured, realizing what he had done. "I should have thought of that."

He leaned over her and kissed her. "I would never risk hurting you."

She ran her hands down his back, pulling him closer, feeling his heavy weight along her thigh. She reached for him, running her fingers along his hard length. "I know that."

He nuzzled her neck. "Do that again and this won't take very long."

"I don't want to wait." She didn't want to wait another minute to have him inside her. He entered her swiftly, a hard smooth motion that made her gasp.

He hesitated. "Am I hurting you?"

"No," she managed to say. Her fingers smoothed his hips, memorizing the feel of his body underneath her hands. "No," she repeated, as he moved partially out of her to plunge into her again. He lifted himself slightly, putting his weight on his elbows as he looked down into her face.

"I love watching you," he said, moving in and out of her with deep, compelling strokes.

She wanted to smile, but he filled her again, and her body welcomed every silky thrust. They blended as if they'd been lovers for years, with no sense of strangeness or awkwardness. It was as if he knew when to slow down, when to tease, when to go deep and hard. When she tightened around him, climaxing in waves of pleasure, he followed her, his hoarse cry echoing hers. She felt his heart beat as rapidly as hers until, after long moments, their breathing slowed and steadied.

He rolled onto his side, taking her with him, and smiled into her eyes. "That was even better than I remembered."

She smiled back. "Must be the moonlight."

"Or the champagne."

She wriggled against him. "I have some bad news for you."

He shook his head. "As long as you're in this position there's no such thing as bad news."

"That's the point." She chuckled. "I think we rolled over on the cake."

His eyebrows rose, and he slid his hand down her body to her hips, reaching underneath their joined bodies. "I think you're right."

She lifted her hip and he shoved the paper plate aside. "So much for dessert."

He gave her a wicked grin. "That means you have frosting on your—"

She put her hand over his mouth, stopping his words. "Yes."

He kissed her palm, until she removed her hand and smoothed it over his jaw. He carefully withdrew from her.

Anne started to sit up. She hated to leave, but she realized she needed time to shower and change before the show ended and Martha returned home.

"Not yet," Chris murmured. His lips touched her abdomen, then lower, to the sensitive skin between her thighs. "I haven't had dessert."

"Chris—"

"Don't tell me to stop," he whispered.

She could barely hear his words over the sound of the waves.

"It would be impossible anyway."

His tongue sampled each delicate fold, sending heated waves along her skin until she melted against his mouth. He tasted every inch of her, his hands cupping her buttocks to hold her still against his mouth, until the sensations took her to a place she'd thought she'd never feel again, and she shattered against his mouth.

9

"COME ON DOWN," Dan insisted, his words muffled by the sound of the crowd in the background. "I have a surprise for you."

Anne turned from the phone and looked at the kitchen clock. Almost eleven. She'd just stepped out of the shower and put on her nightgown. "I can't. I'm not dressed."

"Change," Dan said.

"Where's Martha?"

"With me." His voice faded, then came back strong. "Actually, she's getting a soda at the bar."

"Dad, for heaven's sake!"

"Don't worry. It's perfectly harmless. She's with little Jessie and her mother. Come on, it'll be fun. You've only been to the cabaret once, haven't you?"

"Yes, but—"

"This is going to be different."

Right. Her eleven-year-old daughter was in a lounge, hanging out with the actors, when she should be brushing her teeth and getting ready for bed. Anne glanced down at her nightgown. "Give me a few minutes to change."

"That's my girl!"

He hung up the phone, leaving Anne holding a silent receiver and wondering what her father was up to now. With Dan McNally one just never knew.

After the scene on the beach three nights ago, she'd intended to spend less time at the theater. The fact that Chris had called the next day to tell her he had to go to New York had made it easier to stay away from the place. Easier to deal with the fact that she'd fallen in love with him again.

Making love with Chris had always been an experience. And falling in love with him had always been easy. Too easy. Resisting him was the difficult part. Especially when she remembered the way his body fit with hers, and the sleek, heated feel of his skin as they'd made love on the soft blanket.

Anne banished the memory and hurried back to her bedroom and pulled on a pair of white jeans and a black T-shirt, then hurried to the bathroom to blow-dry her damp hair.

The emcee had already introduced the first singer, one of the dancers from the show, when Anne walked through the lounge and opened the connecting door between the two rooms. The elderly man at the reservations desk recognized her and pointed to a square table off to one side of the room, where Marie sat alone, so Anne wove through the crowded tables and quietly slid into a chair next to Marie.

When the song was finished, Anne applauded and turned to Marie. "Where are they?"

Marie knew exactly whom she meant. "They were here a few minutes ago, but they've disappeared. Dan told me to wait here." She smiled. "I never know what that man is going to do next."

"I know what you mean."

"What a life you must have had," Marie said. "All that excitement, all those wonderful places you've lived and the people you've met."

"I never knew where we were going to be one month to the next," Anne said.

"How exciting! I really envy you that kind of childhood."

Anne shook her head. "Parts of it were fun, but I dreamed of living in one place and never ever leaving."

Marie shook her head. "The grass is always greener, I guess. My kids grew up in the same house they were born in, and both of them couldn't wait to get out and see the world. They haven't stopped."

"How old are they?"

"Bob is twenty-nine and Laura will be thirty-two next month."

"Are you a grandmother?"

"Not yet, but I can't wait. I envy Dan his relationship with Martha."

"They spend a lot of time together, especially since the rehearsals started."

"Your father is an incredible person. He's so full of life."

"He's always been that way," Anne agreed. "Except after my mother died. He went into a slump for over a year. I was really worried about him, but *The Music Man* has cheered him up."

"It's not easy to lose someone you love," Marie agreed. "My husband died five years ago—cancer—and it was very hard to want to go on without him."

"I'm sorry."

"I have my work—*both* jobs." She smiled. "And they keep me busy. Your father has been a good friend."

"I'm glad," Anne replied, and she meant it. After all, her mother would have wanted Dan to be happy, to return to the stage and do what he loved to do. Even if that meant dating again.

"I think we're about to see the surprise," Marie announced, nodding toward the stage.

Anne turned to see her father and Martha stepping on the small stage in front of the fieldstone fireplace.

"Cast of tonight's show," finished the announcer. "Let's give them a big round of applause."

Martha adjusted the height of the microphone stand as if she'd been doing it all of her life while the audience clapped. "My grandfather and I would like to sing a little something for you." She looked over to Dan, who stood waiting in front of his microphone.

"Hit it, honey," he said, and the audience chuckled as the piano player gave them the opening notes.

Anne leaned forward, trying to see over the head of the elderly woman seated at the table in front of her as Dan began to sing the first line of "Me and My Shadow."

They charmed the audience, and when they were done with the popular duet, applause took over. Martha grabbed her grandfather's hand and tugged him from the stage. His reluctance to leave only made the audience laugh more, as he knew it would. It was an act Anne had seen her parents do a thousand times. She watched them join the others near the stairs and accept their congratulations before winding through the tables to join them, flushed and triumphant.

"Well?" Dan whispered, sliding into the seat beside Marie. "What do you two think about our surprise?"

"You both were wonderful," Marie said.

Anne shook her head and smiled. "I should have known you wouldn't stop at playing the constable."

He put his arm around Martha and hugged her to him. "My new partner is pretty good, isn't she?"

"A natural," Anne had to agree. "But it's a little late, so we're going to—"

"It's in the blood," someone with a deep voice interrupted.

Anne felt a hand on her shoulder and knew instantly who stood behind her. He didn't give her time to turn around, but slipped into the empty chair between her and Marie.

There wasn't time to say anything, because the next act was introduced as one of the stagehands took a guitar and sang a funny song about Rhode Island politics. Anne listened politely, but it was hard to concentrate on the song with Chris sitting so close to her. The last time she'd seen him she'd been wearing a silly grin and a lot of sand as she'd climbed into her car to drive home. It hadn't been easy washing the sand off her body. The thought brought color to her cheeks, color she hoped no one noticed. Marie gave her an odd look. So Anne turned to Chris as the guitarist took a bow and left the stage.

"I didn't know you were back."

"I got in a couple of hours ago, in time for the second half of the show," he whispered. "Would you like something to eat? I can call the waitress over."

Martha nodded. "Could I have one of those ice-cream sundaes with the cookie on the bottom?"

"No," her mother said. "We're heading home."

"Already?" Martha cried, hoping her grandfather would come to her rescue.

"Already?" Chris echoed. "I haven't seen either one of you in days. Could you stay a little longer?"

"Don't look at me," Dan told his granddaughter. "I'm staying out of this one."

"Please, Mom? Becky's going to sing tonight, I think, and Grandpa might do another song if they need him to."

Chris chuckled and waved to one of the young waitresses. "Sounds like you're outvoted, Annie. Want dessert?"

"I'm the mother," she explained. "I *can't* be outvoted."

No one made a move to leave the table. The waitress came over, her pad ready. "What can I get you, Mr. Bogart?"

He turned to Anne. "Glass of white wine?"

"All right." Mother or not, she was outvoted.

"SOMETHING SMELLS GOOD," Dan said, stepping into the kitchen. He poured himself a cup of coffee from the pot and eyed his daughter.

"Zucchini bread," she said, wiping off the counter with a sponge. "I want to talk to you, Daddy."

"You sure like zucchini." He edged toward the back door.

"Don't try to change the subject, and don't leave." She turned on the faucet and rinsed the sponge. "We have to talk about last night."

Dan sighed, and sat down at the kitchen table. "We're just friends."

"You should have talked to me about—" Anne turned, realizing what he'd just said. "What?"

"Talked to you about what?"

"About Martha singing in the cabaret. What are *you* talking about?"

He gulped. "Dating Marie."

"That's none of my business," Anne admitted. She sat down at the table across from him. "I have an opinion, of course." He didn't say anything. "Are you really just friends?"

"Of course."

He didn't sound convincing. "She's a very nice lady. I like her."

"You do?" He looked up from his coffee cup. "I thought you'd be upset that I was seeing someone."

Anne put her hand over his, willing him to look at her. "We both miss Mom, but I know she wouldn't have wanted you to spend the rest of your life alone."

"And what about you?"

Anne frowned. "We're not talking about me, Daddy."

"We are now." He gave her hand a squeeze. "If it makes you feel any better, I talked to Chris before Martha and I sang last night. He thought it was a fine idea, as long as we were one of the first ones so Martha wouldn't stay up later than she had to."

"You should have talked to *me*."

"The man wants to be a father, honey. I thought it was about time he started acting like one."

"That's not your decision to make."

"I can see that." He winked, the charming McNally wink that so delighted the audiences of *My Fair Lady*. "You should be doing more than baking zucchini bread, darlin'. You should be spending time with Christopher. That man is in love with you."

"We're still attracted to each other, I suppose." *We're still more than willing to rip our clothes off and make love in the dunes.*

"It's more than that," Dan argued. "You're in love with him, too. It's written all over your face. Do you think I'm blind?"

"Aren't we off the subject? I don't want Martha singing in the cabaret."

"Why not? It's harmless."

"It's too late at night."

"She's sleeping late."

"It's almost eleven o'clock. She should be outside playing with the girls next door, or getting ready to go to the beach with me."

"You're not getting ready to go to the beach. You're baking bread."

"I'm killing time."

"No, you're not," he argued. "You're always cleaning or weeding or baking or something domestic, like some sort of 1950s television mother."

Anne laughed. "I am not!"

"I'm glad you're happy, but for heaven's sake, Annie. Have some fun. Martha's little part in *The Music Man* isn't going to ruin her life, and singing in the cabaret once in a while isn't going to keep her from getting enough rest. Besides—" He took a sip of his coffee before continuing. "We were a hit."

Anne stood. "And that's all that matters? That you were a hit?"

Dan looked at her, a blank expression on his face. 'We had fun, Annie. That's all. Have you forgotten what that's like?" He took his coffee and left the room, and Anne heard the front door open and close, meaning he'd taken his coffee out to the front yard. He liked to sit on the step and look at the distant ocean.

The buzzer on the oven went off, filling the kitchen with its annoying warning before Anne could turn it off. She hadn't wanted to argue with her father; she'd just wanted him to understand he had to talk to her first before involving Martha in any more activities at the theater.

She opened the oven and inspected the two loaves of bread. Heavy with grated zucchini and spiced with cinnamon, their fragrance filled the kitchen. Anne removed them from the oven and placed them on racks to cool. She was sorry she'd hurt his feelings. Maybe a slice of warm bread would make it up to him.

She took a serrated knife out of the top drawer and cut off a thick slice from the end of one loaf. As soon as Martha woke up, they'd pack a picnic lunch and go to the beach for the rest of the day. Maybe Dad was right. Maybe she had forgotten how to have fun.

"JUST THE WOMAN I wanted to see," Chris said, as Anne walked up the stairs to the front porch of the theater. An hour before the show started, the grounds were quiet. Except for the actors' cars, the parking lot across the road was empty.

She wished he wouldn't say things like that. "Why?"

"I missed you." He smiled. "You didn't stay at the cabaret long enough for me to tell you that, and when I stopped by your house this afternoon you weren't home."

She wished he didn't look quite so handsome. "Martha and I went to the beach."

"You're supposed to say you missed me, too."

Her eyebrows rose. "Is that in the script?" He nodded, so she repeated, "I missed you, too."

He shook his head. "Put a little more heart into it, sweetheart. I'm having trouble believing you."

"I'm not the actress in the family."

"You didn't miss me, not even a little?"

"Shh." She glanced toward the box office. "Someone will hear you."

"Why does that bother you?" When she didn't answer he took her elbow and ushered her into the garden area. "Never mind. I can tell you want me to change the subject."

"I'm trying to be professional," she explained, inhaling the scent of roses as they stopped in a sheltered overhang of vines and petaled flowers.

"And I'm trying to kiss you," he murmured, pulling her against him. "Any objections?"

"Hundreds," she replied, lifting her face to his as his lips neared. "Maybe more."

His fingers reached to tangle underneath her hair, his mouth meeting hers in a demanding kiss designed to still her protests and silence her words. She met him with a hunger of her own, wrapping her arms around his neck to hold his mouth against hers for long, heated moments. Finally, when he released her, she stepped away and slid her hands away from him as if they'd never touched.

"I need your help," he said finally.

"With what?" Her heart slowed its rapid pace.

He took a deep breath. "The staff clambake. We do it every August."

"Sounds like fun." *Fun.* That word again.

"I was hoping you'd say that. I wondered if you'd help me plan it."

She should stay as uninvolved with his life as she could. Sex was one thing, neat and compartmentalized into an unavoidable passion that could be ignored in the daylight hours. But becoming part of his world was dangerous. "What do you want me to do?"

"Is that a yes?"

"No. That's a question."

"Help me plan the menu. The crew here at the restaurant will cater it, but I could use some help deciding what to feed everyone."

That didn't seem like much to ask. "All right," she agreed. "I'm not sure how much help I'll be, but—"

"Great!"

Anne backed up, ready to head inside. "Well, I have to go. We clean up under the seats before the show."

"Are you working both shows?"

"Yes."

"Have dinner with me in between shows, then. You work up until after intermission, so you're free from six o'clock until about eight, right?"

"Right." She tried to resist—really she did. It wasn't as though she'd had a lot of practice, though.

"Martha and Dan eat with the cast in the lounge, don't they?"

"Yes." The restaurant provided a buffet for the cast in between the two Saturday shows, an event Martha looked forward to.

"I've missed you," he said, lowering his voice. "I keep remembering Tuesday night, and wishing we were alone."

"Me, too," she admitted, glancing around to make sure no one was within hearing distance.

"Tell me," he demanded, leaning closer. "Or I'll kiss you right now."

"Oh, all right. I missed you."

His pleased smile threatened to take her breath away. His eyes twinkled. "I think I'll kiss you anyway."

She backed up. "Oh, no, you won't. Martha and my father are around here somewhere."

"You don't want Martha to know?"

Anne shook her head. "I don't want her getting any ideas about us."

He frowned, staring down at her. "I never know what you're thinking or why."

"Hey, Chris!" Denny stepped around the corner. "The barbershop quartet is complaining again, and—" He stopped and grinned. "Hi, Anne. Am I interrupting something?"

"Not at all," Anne assured him. "I was just going to work."

"Brace yourself for a crowd. Both shows are sold out, and the rest of them are going fast."

"Then I'd better get busy. I'll see you both later." She turned and hurried toward the stairs.

Denny eyed Chris. "You should look happier. We have a hit."

"I've got woman trouble," Chris muttered, watching Anne disappear around the front of the theater.

His friend grinned. "You've never had any trouble with women before."

"This one's different. Special."

"How do you know?"

"That's the trouble, pal," Chris said, still frowning. "I've always known. I just don't know what the hell to *do* about it."

IT TOOK HIM ONLY until intermission to come up with an idea. He was tired of playing by Anne's rules. The last time he'd run things his way they'd ended up where they should be: in each other's arms. Anne wanted to avoid admitting that there was anything out of the ordinary between them, but when they'd made love to each other there was more to it than just the joining of bodies for a quick, physical release. He wanted her more than he'd ever wanted a woman before, but it wasn't simply sex.

And it wasn't just for the summer. Everything changed after he'd held her, after he'd made love to her. He wasn't going to let her go come September. He'd made that mistake once before, and look what it cost him. No, there was more going on here than a simple summer romance, whether Anne realized it or not.

Chris waited until the crowd, accompanied by music, settled into their seats once again, before approaching Anne. She stepped into the lobby and pulled the curtain into place before moving quietly toward him.

"You *did* agree to dinner, didn't you?"

"I don't remember what I agreed to," she whispered.

"You kissed me as if you were agreeing to something."

She smiled. "I suppose I did. Wasn't that about the clambake?"

"No." He took her arm. "Quit teasing," he said, noting her smile. "I'm hungry."

"What's the special tonight?"

"I have no idea." He tugged her right when she would have turned left. "We're going to my house," he explained. "You're concerned about privacy, right?"

She didn't answer immediately. "Well, yes."

They were soon out of the light and into the darkness that led to his driveway. "And I agree with you. It's no one's business," he said, guiding her up the stairs.

"I feel like I'm skipping school," she confessed.

"Feels good to run away, doesn't it?" He dropped her hand to unlock the door. As soon as they were both in the dark house he took her into his arms.

"I want you all to myself."

Which was the way it had always been, Anne realized. The flush of happiness at his words gave way to a pang of longing to go back to the way it was, to do it over again. Only this time there would be no goodbyes, no heartbreak and no sad, pregnant days of loneliness and fear.

Just the two of them, sneaking off to be together. The years dropped away once more, revealing two people who couldn't keep their hands off each other.

She wrapped her arms around him; he backed her up against the unadorned wall that separated the dining area from the entry. His mouth took hers, in a hungry melting kiss that would have knocked her to the floor if his hands hadn't held her waist. He leaned into her, and Anne welcomed the heavy weight against her thighs.

She couldn't resist squirming against him. "You planned this, didn't you?"

He kissed her neck, parting her collar. His hands moved to unbutton her blouse. "All the way home on the train."

"Must have been a long trip." She tugged his shirt from his pants and slid her hands along the smooth skin of his back. "What about dinner?"

"Later."

"Good." She unsnapped the clasp at his waistband with impatient fingers.

"Much later," he groaned.

"Even better," she managed to reply.

His hands were on her breasts, pushing the lace aside to allow his lips to touch the soft skin that swelled against his touch. They sank slowly to the wooden floor, a tangle of half-clothed bodies and warm skin. He slipped out of his dark slacks and pulled her on top of him. She pushed her skirt up to her waist and wriggled her underwear off while he caressed one breast with his tongue.

"Wait," he moaned, reaching for his pants. "This is one summer that's not going to end like the last one did."

When he was ready, he grasped her hips and lifted her on top of him with one smooth motion. She took him easily inside of her, tight and slick and ready. Neither one noticed the hard floor underneath them as they moved together in a perfect, tantalizing rhythm. Chris protected her from the hard floor, cradling her body against his, yet moving inside of her, as she took his entire length within her over and over again. And when she cried out and convulsed around him, his fingers gripped the softness of her buttocks and held her tightly while he found his own release. She collapsed against his chest and lay there until the earth seemed to drift back to where it belonged, and the only sound in the dark house was their quiet breathing and the rhythmic chirp of a cricket. They lay together for long, peaceful moments, listening to the sound.

"I read somewhere," Chris said softly, his breath fanning her cheek as she lay on his chest, "that having a cricket in your house is a sign of good luck. The Chinese give a cricket box to newlyweds to guarantee good fortune in their home."

"You have a very loud good-luck charm, then," she murmured, wondering if she should move and knowing she wasn't capable of it.

His hands smoothed her back in a loving gesture. "I wouldn't argue with my good luck," he whispered.

"NEXT TIME we use a bed," Chris declared, climbing the steps to the lobby.

"Shh," Anne warned. They'd had enough time to shower and make an omelet before returning to work the next show, but Anne hoped the wrinkles on her skirt wouldn't be noticeable. It was linen, after all, and supposed to look wrinkled, but this was ridiculous.

"Where have you been?" Dennis hurried up to them. He looked at Chris. "I've been searching everywhere for you."

"What's up?"

"The computer just crashed in the box office, and Liz is tearing her hair out. And Sally's having problems backstage with the kids."

"What kind of problems?" Anne asked.

"They're just being too noisy. We're going to need someone back there to keep an eye on them and calm them down if they get too excited and start making noise." He looked hopefully at Chris. "You want to do it?"

"I will," Anne offered. "That is, if you'd like me to."

"If you think you can handle it."

She smiled. "I'm a high-school teacher."

Dennis nodded. "Great. I'd appreciate the help. Just go backstage when you're through seating people." He glanced at his watch. "I'd better tell them to open the doors now."

Chris touched Anne's shoulder. "Will you stay for the cabaret? I think your father signed up to sing."

She resisted the urge to touch him. "Not tonight." At his disappointed look, she added, "Come have breakfast with us tomorrow. Anytime after ten."

"Sounds good. I'll bring the Sunday paper and a bag of doughnuts from the market."

He seemed to want to kiss her, so Anne stepped away. "I'd better get back to work before Marie fires me."

"Good luck," he said, allowing her to move away from him. "I'll meet you backstage in a little while."

By the time she'd slipped through the back door to the small backstage area, the actors had positioned themselves on the train, ready for the curtain to go up. Her father's eyebrows rose when he saw her, and he motioned for her to stand beside him near the stairs.

"Decided to see the show from a different angle?"

"Dennis asked me if I'd try to keep the kids quiet," she replied. "Where are they?"

"The girls are upstairs, I think. Adam should be around here somewhere." He eyed her again. "You look good. Wearing makeup tonight?"

"Uh, no."

"You're glowing," Dan persisted. "You must have had a little wine at dinner?"

Anne didn't have to answer, because the music began and the curtain opened. The cast assembled backstage, all of them whispering the lines under their breath.

"Cash for the merchandise," they chanted, grinning at each other, while the actors onstage relayed their lines in precise time to the music.

When it was over, Dan grabbed Anne's arm and pulled her onto the narrow stairway.

"We have to get out of the way of the train," he cautioned. "They're going to push it back here, then move it out during intermission."

Anne watched as the stagehands maneuvered the sets into place. The audience voiced their approval over the "Iowa" scene.

"Cover your ears," Dan said, doing the same.

She did as she was told, and a gun went off. Adam shuffled over to one of the dancers and tweaked her braids.

Anne crooked her finger at him, motioning him over to her. "You have to be quiet," she told him, and he grinned. Jessie and Martha came giggling out of the bathroom. "Girls!" Anne whispered. "Keep your voices down!"

"Mom? What are you doing here?"

"I'm to keep an eye on the three of you to make sure you stay quiet back here. The assistant director's complained about the noise."

"Uh-oh," Adam said.

"That's right," Anne agreed, trying not to smile. "Uh-oh." Martha rolled her eyes while Jessie watched, openmouthed.

As the show went on, Anne could understand why it would be hard for the children to stay calm. She got caught up in the excitement, too, as the various cast members ran on and off the stage. The applause thundered at all the appropriate times; the actor playing the music man had a towel waiting for him after each scene, the "ladies" were helped in and out of their costumes, their hats pinned on carefully so there would be no accidents. Her father sang and danced in the crowd scenes, actors strolled outside for fresh air in between their times onstage and sets rolled in and out, up and down, off and on.

Dan helped the stage crew pick up beans after Becky and Martha's song, the dancers stretched, and soon intermission brought everyone racing backstage for a fifteen-minute costume change, if necessary, and a break.

Chris found her standing on the deck in the back, making sure the kids didn't do anything to hurt their costumes while they jumped around with two of the young women from the dance troupe until the warning bell sounded.

He stood close to her for the rest of the show, laughed as the assistant director made a joke about Adam spitting on the audience when he lisped his lines, and sometimes put his hand on her shoulder, as if to convince himself that she was really there.

They had two curtain calls and a standing ovation, and when Martha skipped offstage, Chris swept her into his arms for a hug.

Dan pounded him on the back. "We did it again," he crowed, his face flushed beneath the makeup as he removed his wide-brimmed hat.

"We have a hit, all right," Chris agreed, beaming at his daughter.

Anne's heart sank. They were in a different place now, a world all their own. A world that had nothing to do with family dinners or houses with gardens or nine o'clock bedtimes. It was a world that came alive after dark, when the spotlight shone on the stage and the music played the opening song.

It was a world in which a career depended on being at the right place at the right time, going wherever the part led and saying goodbye to people and places you'd never have a chance to love.

She looked at Martha, at her sweet happy face as she said something to Chris. She wished she could tell her daughter that this was no life for her, but she wondered if it was too late.

10

"ARE YOU SURE you've had enough sleep?" Chris looked at his watch, then back to his daughter. "You had a very late night."

Martha just grinned at him as she took a seat at the kitchen table. "I'm fine, Chris."

"The French toast will be ready in a minute," Anne told her. She watched Chris frown, determined to be protective and fatherlike.

"Make sure you get enough rest today," he cautioned. "It's the end of a long week."

"I'm going over to play with Nancy and Lisa."

"Who are they?" Chris glanced over at Anne. "Are they nice girls?"

Martha frowned at him. "You feeling all right, Chris?"

"Never better."

Martha shook her head as if to say she'd never figure out directors, then replied, "Of course they're really nice. They go to my school, but they're not in the same grade."

Anne flipped the bread in the frying pan. "They seem like nice kids, but I'll bet there are a lot of good kids around here, Martha. You just have to give them a chance. Maybe when school starts you can start inviting kids over to play after school."

Martha sighed. "Everyone plays soccer or softball or something like that. They're real busy."

"You could do that, too."

"I don't know how."

Chris brightened. "I can teach you how to throw a ball."

Martha shrugged. "I don't know."

"Why not?"

"I'd rather learn tap."

"We can do both," he insisted. "Starting this morning. Right after breakfast."

"Not today," Anne told the child. "Nancy and Lisa are counting on you."

"But—"

"No buts. You've already made plans. Tap dancing and ball throwing can happen another day."

Martha looked over to Chris as if asking for help, but he shook his head.

Anne hid a smile and turned from the stove, the frying pan in her hand. "Breakfast is ready," she announced. "Who's hungry?"

"Me," Martha declared.

"I can wait," Chris offered. "You go ahead."

"I'll wait for the next batch," Anne said, placing two slices of bread on his plate. "Go ahead and start. Help yourself to juice."

"Thanks." He shot her an intimate smile. "This makes two meals in a row we've shared."

Martha stopped pouring maple syrup on her French toast and glanced up at them. "You ate together last night?"

"Yes," Anne said, turning back to the stove so Martha wouldn't see the flush on her cheeks. "In between shows."

"I didn't see you."

"You didn't?" Chris asked. "Where were you?"

"With Grandpa."

"That's why," Chris declared with enough ambiguity to satisfy an eleven-year-old. For once Anne was grateful the man could act so well.

"Oh. Want the syrup?"

He took the plastic bottle. "Thanks."

"So, Mom invited you over for breakfast. Why?"

"She likes me," Chris whispered. "Amazing, isn't it?"

Martha's mouth dropped open. "You mean, you're like, *going out?*"

Chris calmly picked up his knife and fork and began cutting up his breakfast. "Is that such a surprise?"

"Is *what* a surprise?" Dan asked, stepping into the kitchen. "Did I miss something by sleeping late?" He went over to Anne and gave her a quick kiss on the cheek. "Good morning, Annie. I see you're busy at the stove, as usual."

"Good morning, Dad. Want some?"

"Not yet," he said, sitting down at the table in between Chris and Martha. "Good morning."

"Hi, Grandpa."

"'Morning, Dan. You don't look any the worse for singing at the cabaret last night."

"I'm used to these hours." He winked at Martha. "Cabaret gets started an hour early tonight, sweetheart. Maybe we should do our song."

"Chris and Mom are going out," Martha announced.

"That's no problem. I'll bring you home."

"No." Martha sighed. "Chris and Mom are *dating*." When her grandfather looked blank, she added, "*Together*."

"So?"

Anne brought a plate of French toast to her father, silently thanking him for acting as if this were no big deal. "Here," she said. "Eat it while it's hot." She looked at the others. "Who wants seconds?"

"*So?*" Martha repeated, her hazel eyes wide. "Am I always the last one around here to know anything?"

"That's enough," Anne cautioned. "Some things are none of your business."

"My mother is dating my director and it's none of my business," Martha muttered. "Right."

Chris pushed his empty plate away. "You have some objections?"

"Well, no."

"Then what's the problem?"

Martha shrugged. "I thought you were just friends. Now it's like there was a secret and I was left out."

"I would never want you to feel left out," Chris said, his voice soft. He smiled at her, then up at Anne. "Right?"

Anne stared at him, hoping he was remembering their agreement to tell Martha the truth *after* the show was finished. "Right. And it wasn't a secret."

Martha didn't appear convinced, but she smiled. "Can I sing tonight?"

Anne hesitated. "I don't—"

"Tomorrow's our day off," Dan added.

Anne looked at Chris for help, but he just grinned. "They were a big hit last time," he reminded her. "And it *is* an early night."

"I guess I'm outvoted again."

"Sit down and eat," Chris said, pulling out a chair for her. "You'll feel better, and we'll talk about what we're going to do today."

"We will?" She fixed her plate and approached the table. An erotic vision of what was possible floated through her mind.

"Sure. Let's act like tourists and go to Galilee and eat clam cakes and look at the ocean."

So much for erotic visions. Anne picked up her fork. "Sounds like fun. Anyone else interested?"

Martha shook her head. "I've been invited next door, remember?"

"And Marie and I have plans," Dan said. "She's coming over here and we're going to grill some steaks before work."

"It's hard to believe this show is half over."

"I'm going up to New Hampshire next week," Chris said, "to see if it's feasible to take shows to a regional theater up there for two weeks, after their run here."

"Makes sense," Dan said. "What shows are you doing next year?"

"We haven't made any final decisions, but we're looking at *South Pacific* and maybe *Annie Get Your Gun.*"

Dan whistled. "Sticking with the musicals, are you?"

"The audience loves them," Chris said. "They seem to pretty much guarantee a full house. We're even thinking about putting together something for the road this winter."

Dan's eyebrows went up. "You'll let me know if there's a part for an old hoofer like me?"

Anne couldn't believe her ears. "I thought you'd only come out of retirement for the summer."

He winked at Chris. "A man can always change his mind."

"Yes," Anne answered. "I've heard."

"You'll be the first to know," Chris told him. Then he turned to Anne. "Want to go to New Hampshire with me?"

"I DON'T KNOW how you talked me into this."

"It was easy," Chris announced, glancing at her. "I used my incredible charm and powers of persuasion until you were worn down and couldn't say no. How many miles on 295 before we should get on 95 North?"

She squinted at the map. "Not long. We'll be looking for signs to Worcester."

"That's easy enough."

"I still can't believe I'm doing this." She stared out the window as they passed by trees at an alarming rate.

"You're going to hurt my feelings if you keep saying things like that." He grinned at her. "And I have very tender feelings."

"No, you don't. Actors are the toughest people I know. You automatically bounce back from rejection."

"Maybe I'm the exception."

She dropped the map between them and leaned back against the comfortable seat. "My daughter has never seen me go out with anyone before. I don't know what she's thinking."

"*Our* daughter thinks this is 'cool.' She told me."

"She did?"

"At least three times, while you were still obsessing in the kitchen."

"I wasn't obsessing. I just wanted to make sure there was enough food and that Dad would remember to water the garden."

"We're only going to be away for one night."

"I know."

"And Martha will be fine. Marie is going to be at the house today until it's time for them to go to the theater. They'll have dinner there tonight, and we'll be home tomorrow afternoon. Did I tell you the hotel has a special Sunday brunch?"

"No, but that sounds nice." Safer to think about food than sex.

He reached over and took her hand. "We have twenty-four hours together, Annie. Just the two of us."

Exactly what she didn't want to think about. "Don't we have to visit a theater?"

"Briefly." He put his hand back on the wheel as the traffic thickened around them. "It won't take much time. We'll be at the hotel long before dinner. And there's an indoor pool and an outdoor pool, if you'd like to swim."

"I'd like that." Anne began to relax. The trip really did sound like fun, and so different from anything she usually did. Of course, going overnight with a man was about as opposite to her life-style as anything she could think of. Her husband had never been enthusiastic about quiet weekends away unless his destination contained a golf course. Now she was on her way to an intimate overnight with a man she was in love with. Her daughter would be well cared for, and she had no responsibilities, at least for the next twenty-four hours.

So, why was she so nervous?

"Why are you so nervous?" Chris asked, turning down the volume on the cassette player. The cast recording of *Phantom of the Opera* faded. "This is supposed to be fun."

"I know." She turned, as much as her seat belt would let her, to face him. "And it will be, I'm sure."

"How can it miss?" He fixed his attention on the road, whistling along with "The Music of the Night."

How could she explain to him that she had the awful feeling she was growing accustomed to loving him, eating with him, making love to him, even working with him? He'd become part of her life without her being aware of it.

Only now she was aware. Too aware. A cozy weekend in a New Hampshire hotel would bring their relationship to a different level. From the "remember when" memories of two young people with their lives ahead of them, to an older and wiser couple with careers and a child. And responsibilities. And now those two people were coming together to make love and share a few hours of their carefully hoarded free time.

Anne studied Chris's strong profile, admiring the confident way he moved the car through the traffic. It was going to be all right. He would never have to know how much she loved him, or how much this time together meant to her.

"I HAVE DIED and gone to heaven."

"Now who's being dramatic?"

Anne gazed reverently at the remains of the lobster shell sprawled across her plate. "I love to eat out."

"I'm catching on," he commented, picking up his wineglass. "You must have worked up an appetite in the pool."

"You're not supposed to comment on a lady's appetite," she informed him, dipping the last bite of lobster meat into the bowl of melted butter. "Besides, it's not as if you ordered something light yourself."

He took a swallow of wine, then put down his glass and eyed the empty plate that had held a slab of prime rib. "Looked good, didn't it?"

"If you say so." She turned her attention back to her plate and found one more bit of lobster meat. "This was fun. In fact, this whole day has been fun."

"Good. That was the point."

"Thank you."

He seemed surprised. "You don't have to thank me," he sputtered. "I just wanted to be alone with you."

"You've gone to a lot of trouble to make everything special." From the moment they'd driven up to the mammoth brick building, she'd known she was in a special place. The Nashua Hotel was built to resemble a castle, its luxurious interior designed for elegance. Chris had checked in, then ushered her inside a room on the top floor. A king-size bed dominated the huge room, then Chris opened the drapes to reveal a view of the sloping lawn and duck pond they'd passed driving into the parking area. He'd left her alone to change for dinner, and when he'd returned he'd put on a tie and sport coat and led her to the dining room.

He smiled, the twinkle in his eyes leaving no doubt where his thoughts lay. "And I'm not through yet."

She smiled and picked up her wineglass. "I didn't think you were."

"I've never made love to you in a bed," he whispered. "We've never spent the night together, and I've never awakened in the morning with your face beside mine on the pillow."

It all sounded wonderful, especially the bed part. "What should I do if you snore?" she teased.

"Maybe I don't plan to sleep."

The waiter appeared and cleared their plates. "Would you care to see our dessert cart?"

Anne shot Chris an inquiring look.

"Go ahead," he urged. "Enjoy yourself."

"Thank you," she told the waiter. "I'd like a cup of tea, also."

"And a brandy for me," Chris said.

"No dessert?" Anne asked, as the waiter whisked the remnants of their dinner from the candlelit table.

He gave her his sexiest smile. "I'll have mine later."

She couldn't help responding to his smile. The man positively exuded sex appeal. His charm had transcended the stage and captivated the audiences that summer, leaving everyone who'd experienced the Bogart magic no doubt they'd witnessed the birth of a star. "Are you sure you don't miss being onstage? You never wanted to do television or movies?"

He shook his head. "*Everyone* wants to do movies," he said. "And I did quite a few, just small parts, nothing memorable. But I missed New York and the excitement of live theater."

"And now you own your own."

"Which is the best of both worlds," he said, thanking the waiter for the brandy placed at his elbow. "Just like this weekend."

"I see what you mean," she said, watching the waiter wheel a cart full of desserts toward their table. "This shouldn't even be legal."

"Take your time," Chris said as she eyed the selection on three tiers of glass shelving. "We have all night."

WE HAVE ALL NIGHT. The words echoed in her head as they took the elevator to the seventh floor and walked silently, hand in hand, toward the room at the end of the long corridor. Chris unlocked the door to reveal the dim light of a bedside lamp and the bed turned down at the corners, foil-wrapped mints placed on the over-size pillows to indicate the maid had prepared the room for the evening.

We have all night. He hung the Do Not Disturb sign on the doorknob and bolted the door behind them, keeping her hand firmly in his as if he couldn't bear to let her go.

She parted her lips as he bent close to kiss her, a sweet brandy-seasoned caress that seemed to last forever, as he held her against him. He reached for the hem of her white skirt, sliding his hands up her thighs inch by tantalizing inch. She sighed, loving the feel of his lips, the taste of him in her mouth. His fingers slid higher, to caress her hips through the silk fabric of her underwear.

"Not yet," she said, stepping back from the embrace. He seemed ready to protest, until she added, "You first." She tugged his sport coat down his arms and hung it carefully in the closet while Chris stood in the middle of the room and looked amused.

Then she reached for his tie, untangling the knot with smooth motions, kissing the soft skin of his neck above his collar before unbuttoning his shirt. She took her time, kissing her way down his bare chest as she released the white buttons and slid the material from the waistband of his beige slacks.

"Anne," he managed to say, reaching for her.

"No." She shook her head, whispering against his chest as she bent to release the waistband of his slacks. "It's my turn. And didn't you say we have all night?"

He didn't answer, just expelled his breath as she unzipped his pants and slipped small, seeking hands along the waist of his silk boxer shorts. She touched the paisley material. He was hard under her hands, satin smooth and hot.

"Touch me," he rasped.

"My pleasure." She slipped his clothing down, bent to remove his loafers and socks, then pushed them aside. She knelt before him and kissed her way up his legs until she reached the part of him that ached to be caressed. She took him with her fingers, stroking each hard satin inch. "I've always wanted to do this," she murmured, her lips a mere breath away from the sensitive ridge of flesh. She ran her tongue around the plum-shaped tip until Chris groaned. When she would have taken him into her mouth he reached down and lifted her to her feet.

"Enough," he said. "Now it's my turn."

"You want me to stop?"

"No." He managed a wry smile. "But I want your clothes off." He undressed her slowly, taking his time lifting the black tank top over her head, caressing her breasts through the ebony lace bra until they swelled against his palms, aching for more direct contact with his demanding fingers.

She kicked off her white sandals; he unzipped her skirt and tugged it over her hips. He unhooked her bra and tossed it on the carpet while she slithered out of her underpants.

"No fair," he said. "I wanted to do that."

"Want me to put them back on?"

He ran his hand down her abdomen, his fingers tangled in the curls between her thighs. "No way." He cupped her softness in his large hand for a brief, heart-stopping moment, then scooped her into his arms and carried her to the bed.

"It's not going to be easy doing this slowly," he admitted as he bent over her, his chest brushing her breasts.

"We could alternate," she suggested, reaching for him as he towered over her on the bed. "Fast, slow, fast, sl—"

He laughed, kissing the turned-up corner of her mouth. "Well, we can try."

She wound her arms around his neck and pulled him over her, luxuriating in the feel of his skin on hers. "I'm sure you'll do your best. After all, you said we had all night."

"Yes," he whispered, planting slow kisses along the column of her neck. "And in a bed, too."

She wriggled against the soft mattress, an improvement from last week's hardwood floor. "Nice," she murmured.

"We could get spoiled," he informed her, inching lower to nibble between her breasts.

"No more beach blankets?"

"I love your skin," he said, moving down her body in agonizing slowness.

He made it difficult to think. "No lofts or tarps or floors?"

"Never." His breath tickled her abdomen. "You deserve satin sheets and soft mattresses and acres of pillows."

"I don't want acres of pillows," she managed to say, as his lips found her core and caressed her with tingling, heat-filled motion.

He lifted his head to look at her. "Tell me what you want, Annie."

"I want you," she whispered, wondering if it was love she saw in his eyes. Hoping she was right. Praying that somehow this affair would work between them. "I want you," she repeated. "Inside me. Now."

He moved beside her on the bed and turned her to face him. He lifted her leg over his hip and pulled her close, entering her with a firm stroke that left no doubt that he wanted her, too. His mouth was very close to hers.

"There," he said, filling her. "What else do you want, my love?"

She shook her head, her lips brushing lightly against his. "I think—" she hesitated, as he moved within her "—I have everything I need."

They made it last, moving slowly and spinning out each mind-numbing sensation until the waiting became almost pain, until the blanket lay mounded on the floor, the sheets tangled and pulled from their once-tight corners and the pillows mashed against the headboard. When they found release it was together, in an earth-shattering tremor that threatened to toss them off the bed.

Long moments later, when Anne felt her heartbeat return to normal, she kissed Chris's shoulder and wanted to purr with contentment. "I like this idea of using a bed," she murmured.

He lifted his head and smiled down at her. "I do, too."

"We're going to get spoiled."

"I already am." The expression in his eyes grew serious. "Move in with me, Anne. You can decorate the house any way you want, plant a garden, sleep in my bed."

Anne stared up at him. *Move in with me* was not exactly a declaration of undying love or a proposal of marriage. He must be teasing. "I already have a house. And a bed."

"And my daughter," he added. "Don't forget that."

And my love. Don't forget that. She touched his face, smoothed the dark hair from his forehead before answering. "Let's keep things as they are now," she offered. "Things change when summer ends."

"Nothing is going to change how much I love you," he countered, his body warm against hers. He must have seen the surprise flare in her eyes, because he added, "Don't you know I love you, Annie?"

"You did once."

"I never stopped."

"Neither did I," she admitted, feeling her throat constrict as an unknown emotion threatened to overwhelm her.

He touched the corner of her eye with a gentle kiss. "Then why the tears? We're making progress here, aren't we?"

"Progress?"

"I love you—you love me. We're in a bed." His eyes crinkled at the corners. "Wouldn't you call that progress?"

She wrapped her arms around his neck and pulled his lips to hers. "Yes, that's definitely what I'd call it."

MARIE POINTED to the large platter in the middle of the table. "Have another lobster, Anne."

"No, thanks." Anne tossed her empty paper plate into the garbage can at the end of the long table. "I've already had two, but don't tell anyone."

"They're going to go to waste," Marie cautioned. "We had thirty left over last year."

"What did you do with them?"

"Chris told the ushers to take them home. I ate lobster salad for a week."

"Thanks again for helping Dad take care of Martha last Saturday."

"I enjoyed it. Since I don't have any grandchildren, it was fun to have Martha to visit with. She's such a nice young lady. And so talented!"

"I'm not sure how she'll feel when the show is over. She's loved being part of things around here."

"Eight more shows," Marie said, her voice growing soft. "We'll miss . . . everyone in the cast."

Anne touched her on the shoulder. "I don't think you'll be getting rid of the McNallys that easily, Marie."

Marie shot her an embarrassed look. "I've really enjoyed your father's company," she admitted. "He's a very special man."

"Maybe you can make an usher out of him."

"I don't think so," the older woman said. "He's meant to be on the stage, not in front of it."

"Mom!" Martha ran up, out of breath. "Adam and I won the three-legged race. Now they're finishing the volleyball game. Chris said to tell you he needs you."

"He does?"

Martha took her mother's hand and tugged. "That's what he said."

Anne knew when to give up. Besides, she hadn't had two minutes alone with Chris since the party had started two hours ago. Maybe if she played volleyball she'd have a chance afterward to talk to him. "Okay. What about you, Marie?"

"Dan and I are entered in the pie-eating contest." She made a face. "I haven't figured out how I got myself into that."

"It was probably Dad's idea of a good time. Good luck!"

She and Martha walked around the large workshop to the backyard of the restaurant, where a noisy group gathered around the net. Anne spotted Chris right away, standing at the edge of the crowd with a clipboard in his hand.

He looked up and smiled right into her eyes, then waved her over with his free hand. "Help me, Anne!"

"What's the matter?"

"Tell these crazy people to go eat some more."

She made her way through the crowd and took the clipboard from his hand. The sign-up sheet was filled with names. "Women against men?"

The women cheered, but a couple of the men jeered. Anne handed the clipboard to Becky. "You're in charge. I'm stealing your boss for a little while."

Martha stuck close to Becky. "Can I be on your team?"

"Sure." She winked at Anne. "I'll take care of her."

"Thanks."

Chris took her hand, tugging her away from the crowd. He didn't stop walking until they'd rounded the corner and were protected by the lilac bush. He pulled her into his arms and kissed her thoroughly before releasing her.

He looked pleased with himself. "I've wanted to do that since I woke up this morning."

"I can't believe we were in New Hampshire yesterday."

They'd spent a leisurely morning in bed, in the pool and finally at the hotel's extravagant Sunday buffet. She'd slept alone in her bed last night and hadn't liked it one bit.

"It seems like a week ago," she told him, unwilling to leave the warm circle of his arms.

"Sure you don't want to move in with me?"

"Positive," she said. Although she wanted to sleep with him every night and wake up together every morning, she knew it would never last. One morning he'd be off to New York and the separation, however long or short, would only be the first of many. "I got some good news today."

"What?"

"I was called back for a third interview at the high school. There's an opening in the English department, which is exactly what I'm looking for. They've narrowed the applicants down to five, and I'm one of them."

He frowned. "Are you sure you want to work? I want to contribute to Martha's—"

"I've always taught, Chris. I love it, and I have the same vacations and holidays as Martha does. And I don't want your money. Martha and I do just fine."

He didn't look convinced. "You shouldn't want for anything."

"I don't. Not for anything that matters."

He tightened his arms around her. "No fame and fortune, Annie?"

She tried to smile. "I have everything I want right here. My daughter and my home, and with a little luck a teaching job."

"What about me?"

"For right now, we have each other."

"And that's supposed to be enough?"

"It's enough for me," she said lightly, hoping he wouldn't hear the tremor in her voice. She wanted what she couldn't have, because Chris wasn't going to settle down and start planting tomatoes and making babies and driving children to softball practice.

Dan McNally was never going to retire, and Chris Bogart wasn't going to stay in one place more than three months at a time.

11

THE REST of the week passed quickly. Too quickly, Anne decided, ironing her beige slacks for work. Saturday was a long evening, starting an hour before the five o'clock show and ending sometime after eleven-thirty if she stayed until the end. And, of course, she didn't want to miss one minute of the last performances.

"Thank goodness you're home," Dan McNally said, charging through the front door.

Anne looked up from her ironing. "What's the matter?"

He didn't smile. "We have company."

"Who?"

He didn't reply. "Marty's with him outside. She seemed pretty happy to see him."

"Daddy, what are you talking about?" She turned off the iron and stepped around the ironing board toward the front door. "Who's here?"

"John. He just drove up."

"*John?*" Anne slowed her steps to the door and turned to look back at her father. "My ex-husband John?"

She didn't wait for her father to answer, but hurried to the picture window, leaning over the couch to peek at the front yard. "That's him, all right. Why on earth would he be here in Rhode Island?"

Dan shook his head. "Do you want me to stay or leave?"

"Get out while you can," she advised, moving away from the couch as she saw John follow Martha up the walk to the front door. "I'll fill you in on everything later."

"Hey, Mom," Martha called, opening the screen door. "Guess who's here!"

A short, blond-haired man followed her inside the living room. He wore a bright-blue striped polo shirt and white pants. "Hello, Anne. I hope you don't mind my stopping in."

Stopping in? From California? "Uh, no. I'm just surprised, that's all." She stared at him, realizing he looked exactly opposite from Chris. Short and stocky, whereas Chris was tall and lean. Light and dark. Cool and warm. John's eyes, a pale blue, held very little warmth.

"I told him all about the show, Mom. Can he go? Can we get him a ticket so he can see me?"

Anne hesitated. Martha looked so pleased to have John here, the way she'd always been pleased when he'd shown her the least bit of attention. He'd never been mean, but had treated her with the absentminded attention you'd show an old dog. Someone else's old dog.

And Martha deserved so much more than that. Anne swallowed, and said, "I'll do my best." She glanced at John, who pretended to be interested. "That is, if you'd like to."

"I would," he agreed.

"Goody! Where's Grandpa? I want to tell him—"

"He went outside to, uh, water the garden," Anne said quickly. "Why don't you go find him and tell him we're eating in about ten minutes." She turned to her ex-husband as Martha hurried out the back door. "John, what are you doing in Rhode Island?"

"Business meetings in Boston, then golf in New-port." He glanced around the room, clearly unim-pressed by the surroundings. "This isn't what I pictured when you said you were going to live by the ocean, Anne."

"No?" She bit back a retort, not wanting to start an argument. After all, he'd made the effort to see them, an effort Martha appreciated.

"No." He put his hands in his pockets. "I booked a room down the street, at a bed-and-breakfast inn. There didn't seem to be any motels in the immediate area."

"No, not really. People usually rent summer cot-tages by the week."

Martha ran back in the room. "Can he stay for lunch, Mom? Then we can all go over to the theater to-gether."

"That's a good idea, honey. Why don't you put an-other place at the table. You'll stay, won't you? The first show is at five. I can probably get you in, if you don't mind sitting on a folding chair in the lobby. The show's been sold out almost since the first performance."

"I don't want to put you to any trouble, Anne." John looked embarrassed. "I just wanted to discuss a few things."

"It's no trouble. We have a very late lunch on Sat-urdays because we have to be at the theater by four o'clock."

He looked relieved. "There's time to talk, then. And I have the annual reports from those mutual funds I put you into."

"All right. Martha can show you around while I get lunch ready."

It was one of the strangest lunches Anne had ever experienced. Martha chattered away, oblivious to her mother's discomfort, while Dan ate in uncharacteristic silence. Years ago he'd felt that John had insulted him, and he'd never really forgiven him for it. Her mother had tried to befriend her son-in-law, but John had made it clear that Edie McNally was not the kind of mother-in-law he'd expected as part of his family. "Too flamboyant," he'd commented once.

Fortunately Edie hadn't heard him. She'd gone on-stage to star in a San Diego performance of *Hello, Dolly*. Anne smiled at the memory.

"Do you want help?" Dan asked, edging away from the table.

"No, thanks, Dad. I'll just stack them in the sink and do them tomorrow." She looked at her watch. "We should get ready."

John stood up and thanked her for lunch. "I'd better go change, too," he said. "You said the theater is down this street?" At her nod, he continued, "I'll meet you there around four-thirty. Will that be enough time?"

"Sure."

"I'll bring the papers with me. We can discuss them after the show."

She hesitated. That meant she'd have to cancel her dinner plans with Chris. There was no way around it, though. John was only going to be here for the weekend. "All right," she heard herself agree. "We'll come back here."

CHRIS PULLED Dan aside backstage. "Who was that guy in the lobby with Anne?"

Dan adjusted his constable hat and frowned. "She didn't introduce you?"

"I couldn't get close enough for introductions."

"That was John Winston."

Chris felt his stomach drop. "Her ex-husband?"

"Yes."

"What's he doing here? I thought he lived somewhere in California."

"He had business here on the East Coast."

"Is he staying long?" Chris wished he could leave the backstage area and find Anne, but he was stuck filling in for the stage manager at the last minute. Something about food poisoning or an allergic reaction to oysters. Anne had waved to him, but he'd had no chance to approach her.

"I think he's leaving tomorrow, but she told me if I saw you before she did, I was to tell you that she couldn't have dinner with you."

"Damn." Martha ran up, braids flying behind her, and gave him a quick hug. It made him feel better. After all, no matter what, he was this sweet child's father and nothing could ever change that. And after tomorrow night's show, Martha would know exactly who he was and how much she mattered to him.

If he could only convince Anne to become part of his life permanently. But he couldn't picture her packing up to join him on the road. She wanted to teach and garden, and she'd made it clear that Martha was not going to have the kind of childhood that required suitcases and passports. Although he figured Martha wouldn't mind in the least. After all, she was his daughter.

"Hi, honey," he whispered, capturing one braid and giving it a gentle tug. "You all set?"

"Sure! Did Mom tell you my stepfather was here?"

"I heard."

She grinned. "He's not my *real* father, you know."

Dan began coughing. Chris had no idea how to reply. "He isn't?"

"No, but he's okay. Kinda quiet."

"Boring," Dan muttered so only Chris could hear.

"I hope he enjoys the show." *And gets his ass back to California when it's over.*

"THANKS FOR explaining everything to me," Anne said, handing back the sheaf of papers for John to put inside his briefcase.

"It was no problem." He snapped the leather case shut and set it on the floor beside the kitchen chair. "You need to know these things, even though we're no longer married."

"It's very kind of you to continue to take care of these investments for me." She tried to look at her watch without him noticing. Marie expected her back by eight and it wouldn't be fair to anyone if they were one usher short on the busiest night of the week. "Are you going back to San Diego tomorrow?"

He hesitated. "Yes. That's what I'd planned. Unless . . ."

"Unless?"

"I could talk you into returning with me." He looked very calm as he waited for her reaction, as if he'd suggested they have another glass of iced tea.

"But we're divorced." She wondered if she'd heard him correctly. "I can't go back to California. I *don't* want to go back to the way my life was before."

John smiled, his pleasant smile reserved for clients, she noted.

"This is no life for you, living in this place with your father, your daughter hanging out with actors. She's going to grow up in the insanity you did. I thought you wanted more than that."

"I do, but we're—"

He ignored her protest. "I've my eye on new houses going up by the Santa Ridge Golf Course. Forty-three-hundred square feet, fireplace in every bedroom, view, pool and plenty of room for entertaining."

"That doesn't have anything to do with me, John." Expensive houses and golf courses and entertaining didn't fit her life-style, not anymore.

"Of course it does," he insisted. "We made it work once. We could do it again. I don't have time for dating, and I dislike being divorced. What we had was fine."

"Not exactly, John. I don't think we ever loved each other."

He shrugged, as if to say *so what?* "We had a good life. We were friends."

"Maybe at first we were," she conceded, "but you were never home and . . ." She stopped and looked at him. "I don't want to go over all of this again, John. It didn't work then. It's not going to work now."

He sighed and stood up. "If you're sure . . ."

She stood, too, as he picked up his briefcase. "I'm sure."

"Well, tell Martha I enjoyed the show. She was very good." He started for the door and turned back once again. "I don't approve, you know. Her grandfather's influence isn't necessarily a good one, despite the fact that he means well."

Her anger started to rise. "You don't have the right to approve or disapprove. You never adopted her, remember?"

"I never wanted children, Anne. You always knew that."

He opened the door and left, and Anne stood listening for the sound of the car engine and the crunch of the tires on the driveway. As soon as she was sure he was gone she let out the breath she'd been holding and unclenched her hands.

John Winston had offered her security eight years ago, when she'd thought a permanent home and a family were the two things she needed to make her life complete. She thought she'd learn to love him; he thought he'd make her into the perfect corporate wife. They'd both failed.

Anne hurried out the door and locked it behind her. She walked swiftly down the street, back to the theater. Back to Christopher Bogart. Back to warmth and love.

"I HAVE a seat for you for tomorrow night," Marie whispered. "Chris said you can pick up the ticket at the box office."

"Thanks, Marie." She put her hand over her mouth to cover a yawn. "I don't think I'm going to make it through the whole thing tonight."

"Are you leaving after intermission?"

"I think so." Since her conversation with John, she'd had a pounding headache. All she wanted to do was go home and pull the covers over her head. "What about you?"

Marie smiled. "I've seen the show so many times I know the lines by heart, but I'm still not tired of it. Have you seen the way your father leaps across the stage during the last act? I get the biggest kick out of that." She patted her arm. "You go ahead and leave after we seat these people. I'll get one of the other girls to stay for intermission. You look like you're ready to fall over anyway."

"I am a little tired. I had unexpected company this weekend."

"Dan told me." Marie gave her a sympathetic look. "Is he gone?"

"Yes."

"Good. Speaking of men," she said, her eyes twinkling, "Chris is busy backstage, but he told me to ask you about cabaret tomorrow night. He's reserved a table."

"I can't believe it's the last night, although Dad and Martha both seem to be getting tired."

Marie didn't look happy at the thought.

"Have you seen Chris anywhere around here?"

She shook her head. "Not lately. We talked after the first show, but I haven't seen him since. Martha was with Dan during dinner, so you don't have to worry about her. He said that she and the other kids have an Uno game going, too, so they're staying out of trouble backstage." She gazed past Anne's shoulder. "Looks like they've opened the doors. You take the left aisle with me this time."

From that point on Anne was too busy seating people to worry about what would happen tomorrow night. Dan appeared in the lobby, in his shirt sleeves and makeup but without the old-fashioned jacket and hat he wore onstage. He wove through the crowd toward Anne, who stood at the head of the aisle, holding a stack of programs in her arms.

She raised her eyebrows. "Is everything okay?"

"That's what I was going to ask you," Dan said. "Did John leave?"

"Yes."

Chris entered the doorway, glanced around until he saw Anne and joined them in the lobby. "I missed you at dinner."

"I'm sorry about that," she said, wishing she could throw herself into his arms and hold on tight. "I had company."

"I heard. Martha was thrilled."

"Yes," Anne agreed. "It meant a lot to her."

Dan patted her arm. "I'll see you later. Are you staying for the whole show?"

"I'm pretty tired."

Chris started to put his arm around her, but then seemed to remember they stood in a crowded lobby. "What did he want?"

"Could we discuss this later?"

He frowned, his eyes growing darker. "He wanted you to go back to California with him, didn't he?"

"How did you know that?"

His smile didn't quite reach his eyes. "It's what I would do if I were him."

"You're not him," Anne countered, wishing she could go into his arms. She settled for a tremulous smile as she looked up into his worried face.

"I can't offer you what he can."

"I told him I was very happy with my life exactly the way it is."

"Are you sure about that?"

"Yes," she answered, wondering why he appeared aggravated.

Chris stepped back to allow a young man to give Anne his tickets. "You're not working tomorrow night," he called, moving away so she could do her job.

"Yes, I am. Marie—"

"Will find a replacement. I'm picking you up, and we're going to watch the show together."

"Like real people?" she teased, as she handed the young couple programs.

He shook his head. "Like stage parents."

She started to tell him to keep his voice down, then realized that it wouldn't matter much longer. After *The Music Man* was over, she'd promised to introduce Martha to her father, no matter how much she dreaded it.

"THESE MUST BE the best seats in the house," Anne said, settling into the front row balcony seat, in the exact middle of the row.

"They're the house seats," Chris explained. "For honored guests."

She folded her jacket in her lap. "Is that what we are?"

He took her hand and squeezed it gently. "Of course."

"I think I could see this show a hundred times and still be nervous every time Martha comes onstage."

"I know," he agreed. "It happens to me, too."

"She thinks it's *fun*," Anne groaned. "While I'm sick to my stomach with stage fright."

"You wouldn't have made a very good actress," he commented. "It's a good thing you became a teacher instead."

"By the way, I meant to tell you—"

She was interrupted by Dennis's nightly announcement, informing people that the music was live and there would be no photography or video equipment allowed in the theater. He also added his thanks to the staff and cast on this last performance of *The Music Man* and hoped they would all enjoy the show. Then the orchestra sounded the opening chords, the curtain rose and the "salesmen on the train" began their song.

Anne gripped Chris's hand a few minutes later when Martha appeared at the piano for her scene with Becky. The child's voice had strengthened during the past weeks, and she joined Becky in the song.

"'Good night, my someone,'" they sang, and Anne used her free hand to wipe away the tears that ran down her cheeks, no matter how hard she tried to hold them inside. Martha was clearly her father's daughter, holding the audience in the palm of her hand the way Anne remembered Chris being able to do.

Tonight she would have to decide how to tell Martha who her father was. Despite Martha's obvious attachment to Chris, Anne wondered how she'd take the news that the man was her father and wanted to be part of her life from now on. Anne swallowed the lump in her throat as the audience applauded her child and the lovely Marian.

John had offered them security, but little else. And Chris offered love, but made no promises. They wouldn't know where he would be from one month to the next. Near the end of the play, when Marian told Professor Hill that even though he was leaving, she was grateful for what he had given her, Anne knew exactly what she meant.

Chris would be in Rhode Island in the summertime; she and Martha would have him then. It would be enough, she decided, joining the audience as they gave the cast a standing ovation.

It would have to be.

"I HAVE a surprise for you tonight," Chris said as the lights came on. He reached for her hand. "Come on. I have a table for cabaret. Let's go get Martha."

"She'll need to change."

"It won't take long. We'll wait for her."

They made it through the crowd and down the stairs in record time. "What kind of surprise?" He led her down the empty aisle toward the stage.

He grinned. "You'll have to wait and see."

"Give me a hint."

"No. It's too . . . big for hints."

She started to argue, but the scene backstage stopped her. Actors in various stages of dress were hugging each other, crying or shouting goodbyes.

"Watch out," Chris advised. "The stagehands have to break down this set, then get everything in place for the next show."

Anne looked around, amazed at the speed of the crew. "By Tuesday?"

"Yes. They won't get much sleep between now and then."

"Mom!" Martha ran down the stairs, her cheeks still bright with rouge. She wore her new yellow sundress and white sandals and had brushed her long hair so it hung loose to her shoulders. "Everybody's so sad!"

Anne reached for her. "What about you?"

"Well," Martha said, hugging her around the waist. "I *loved* the show and I'm gonna miss everyone, but Chris says it doesn't have to end. He says—"

"Martha!" Jessie, the child who played the mayor's daughter, ran up, her braids bouncing. "Are you going to cabaret, too?"

"I'm singing," she announced proudly.

"I didn't know you and Grandpa were singing tonight," Anne said, surprised that her father hadn't talked to her about it beforehand.

"I'm not—" Martha began, Chris interrupted her with a strange look.

"Come on, we should make sure we get our table," he urged.

"We'll catch up with you," Anne told him. "Martha has to wash the makeup off."

"I'll wait," he said, as if unwilling to let them out of his sight for more than a minute.

Anne looked around the busy area. "Where's your grandfather?"

Martha shrugged. "I don't know. He left pretty fast. Maybe he wanted to practice his song."

"It's odd that he didn't stick around."

"You'll see him at the cabaret," Chris said, his smile mysterious. "I'm positive of that."

"Is there something going on that I should know about?"

Chris's smile widened. "Oh, you'll find out soon enough."

Dan McNally loved surprises almost as much as being onstage. Anne watched as he took his place behind the microphone and adjusted the height of the stand. The audience applauded loudly and waited for "the constable" to begin his song.

Martha wriggled in her seat between Chris and her mother, then reached for her cola. "He looks kinda nervous," she whispered.

Chris chuckled, but didn't offer an explanation.

"Tonight's a special evening for all of us," Dan said, "but especially for me." He looked offstage to where Marie stood by the door. She smiled and he turned back to the audience, searching for Anne. When he caught her eye he said, "I hope my family will forgive me for making an announcement this way, but it seemed appropriate on the closing performance of the show." He took a deep breath and continued. "This old 'music man' would like to tell you that the local librarian, Marie Jameson, has agreed to marry me. And—"

Applause drowned out what he'd planned to add. Anne sat frozen in surprise for a few seconds, but realized that for the past weeks her father had been happy again. If Marie made her father happy, that's all that mattered. She realized the anxious look on her father's face was directed at her, so she raised her hands to show him she was applauding his announcement and watched his relieved expression.

"Thank you all," he said when the applause died down. "I'd like to sing a special song and dedicate it to my lovely fiancée." The pianist began with the opening chords and Dan McNally sang, "'Love is wonderful, the second time around . . .'"

When he was finished he waved to the audience, winked at Anne and hurried off the platform to join Marie and accept congratulations from the other members of the cast assembled off to the side of the room.

Martha grinned at her mother. "That was *so cool*."

"Yes," Anne agreed, watching her father and Marie head toward them. "It was just like your grandfather to make the announcement onstage."

Chris put his arm over the back of her chair and leaned close. "You approve of dramatic gestures? That surprises me."

"Well, it *was* romantic," she admitted. "And so typical of Dad."

"I'm glad you approve."

"I just want him to be happy."

Chris smiled. "I'll order a bottle of champagne," he told her. "The celebration is just getting started."

12

So THEY CELEBRATED. In between performances by the various members of *The Music Man* cast, they toasted Dan and Marie's happiness with champagne for the adults and ginger ale for Martha. Lenny, the young comedian who'd played Harold Hill's only friend in the show, took the microphone and beckoned to Chris.

"We have another first for you tonight. Our director and boss, Chris Bogart, has something special he'd like to sing for you," he announced.

Anne turned to him in surprise. "Chris, you're going to sing?"

"Something for you," he whispered, standing up. He shot her a quick smile before hurrying to the stage.

Lenny clapped him on the back and handed him the mike. The lights dimmed, and the piano player began the opening chords to a song Anne recognized immediately.

"'Where or When,' by Rodgers and Hart," Anne heard Dan tell Marie. "One of my favorites."

Chris sang the poignant love song and never took his gaze from Anne. When he sang the chorus, the words tugged at Anne's heart. What was he trying to tell her? That they were meant to be together again? Her eyes misted with tears as she listened to the words to the song, sung in Chris's strong baritone. Maybe he was right. Maybe what they had together could last forever.

As the final notes trailed off, the audience applauded their approval, the members of the cast cheering their boss as the lights brightened.

Chris held up his hand. "Hold on. I'm not done yet." He beckoned to Martha, who grinned and stood up.

Anne stopped her. "Where are you going?"

Martha giggled. "Wait and see."

"I'm sure all of you recognize our own Martha McNally, who played Amaryllis in the show." Applause filled the room. "Some of you know her grandfather, the man who earlier announced his intention of marrying our head usher." The audience chuckled. Chris held out his hand and helped Martha onstage. "We like to keep everything in the family around here, don't we, Martha?"

"Yep." Lenny placed another microphone in front of her.

"Now," Chris said, making sure Martha was all set. "We've been practicing a little song for tonight." He looked down at Martha. "Ready, kid?"

"Ready." She grinned at the audience.

"A born performer," Dan whispered. "I've told you all along, haven't I?"

"Shh," Anne said, leaning forward as the music started. She recognized it right away. "Side by Side," an old song that her parents had done early on in their career. Martha belted out her part, her voice filling the room. But the surprise came when she did a little soft shoe across the small stage, keeping perfect time with Chris. When had they found the time to practice a dance routine?

As if reading her mind, Dan leaned across the table after the song ended. "They've been practicing before the show every night. Pretty cute, huh?"

"Yes."

The song ended, and the audience cheered their approval as Chris held Martha's hand and they bowed together.

Once more Anne applauded. So Chris had taught his daughter to dance. Not only dance, but harmonize with him. He'd been determined to be a father, and she couldn't blame him for wanting to be part of Martha's life in any way he could. A father-daughter musical act would naturally be his logical choice.

"Thank you," Chris said, still holding Martha's hand. "I have two more announcements before we bring this evening to a close. Next week *Little Shop of Horrors* starts its three-week run here at Theater by the Sea. We have some incredible special effects, so I hope you'll all come back to see that show. A lot of talented people have worked very hard. *And,*" he paused, a smile lighting his face as he looked toward Anne's table "—I'm very pleased to tell you that this year's production of *The Music Man* was such a hit that we're taking it on the road in January for a three-month, seventy-city tour!" He waited for the applause to die down before adding, "Many of the cast members from this summer's show will be coming with us—at least the ones who want to—so it's not the end of *The Music Man.*"

Anne sat frozen, watching Martha beam at Chris as he held her hand and escorted her off the stage. They joined the others in the corner for hugging and kissing and assorted congratulations. They all looked happy and excited, which of course they would be, she realized. The show must go on, would go on for months.

Chris had held his daughter's hand and announced that the members of the cast who wanted to would be heading across the country in January. She turned to her father, and saw by the expression on his face that he'd been in on it all along. "You knew about this?"

"Chris told me yesterday. They're still negotiating the cities and—"

"And you're going, of course."

Marie put her hand on Anne's arm. "We both are. I'm going to retire from the library and go with them. Chris asked if I would help take care of the children, make sure they keep up with their schoolwork and eat properly." She smiled a little shyly. "It all sounds so exciting."

"Take care of the children," Anne repeated. "Of course."

"Now, Anne," Dan began, a worried expression crossing his face. "I know what you're thinking, but that doesn't mean—"

"Did you see her face?"

Dan nodded. "But that doesn't mean he's taking her with him, not without asking you first."

"He's taught her to dance with him, Daddy." She looked over at the crowd of actors by the doorway. Chris was leaving again, going on the road, just as she had expected. But she hadn't ever thought, not once, that he'd suppose he could take Martha with him. "I'm going to take her home now."

"Talk to Chris first," Dan pleaded.

"I can't." She stood up and grabbed her jacket from the back of the chair. "I'm sorry, Marie." She bent down to kiss her cheek. "I'm very happy for the two of you, really. I hope you'll let me help you with the wedding plans."

"Thank you, Anne. That means a lot to me."

"Don't leave like this, Annie-girl," Dan cautioned. "You should talk to Chris before—"

"No." She shook her head and picked up her purse. "Chris should have talked to *me* before letting Martha think she was going on the road."

Lenny grabbed the microphone. "Thanks, everyone! Hope you all had a great time! Drive home safely!"

She reached Martha's side and put her hand on her shoulder. "It's time to go home, honey."

Martha turned to her and burst into tears. "I don't want to say goodbye to everybody!"

Chris stopped his conversation with the leading man and gave Martha a hug from behind. "Don't worry, peanut. It's not over yet."

"Yes," Anne stated firmly. "It certainly is."

Chris lifted his head sharply. "Anne? What's the matter?"

"This particular actress is retiring from show business." She took Martha by the hand and gently removed her from Chris's embrace. "We're going home now."

Martha wiped her eyes with her free hand. "You didn't like our song, did you?"

"Of course I did." Anne pasted a bright smile on her face. "You were wonderful. But it's after midnight and time to go to bed."

Chris pushed open the dividing door. "I'll take you home."

"No."

He looked at Martha, then back to Anne. "I thought we were going to have a talk."

"No."

"*No?*" His mouth thinned in anger as he followed them through the restaurant and outside to the misty night air. They walked along the cobblestone path to the parking lot in silence.

"Wait in the car, Martha," Chris said. "I need to speak to your mother alone for a minute." Martha gave them a curious look, then climbed into the front seat and shut the door.

Chris took Anne's elbow and hauled her past a row of parked vehicles before stopping. "What on earth is going on here, Anne? I thought we'd agreed to tell Martha that I was her father."

She clenched her fists at her side, willing herself not to cry. "Yes, as soon as 'the curtain comes down on the last show.' I think those were your words."

He narrowed his eyes. "You didn't like our song, did you? What's the matter, Anne? Can't you share her just a little bit?"

"A little bit?" she echoed, incredulous. "You stand up there on that stage tonight and announce that you're leaving and you're taking Martha with you and you expect me to *accept* it?"

"I think you're dreaming up excuses to back out on your promise."

"I don't have to 'dream up' anything. There are plenty of reasons to go back to things the way they were."

"What happened to the fact that we love each other?"

"A mistake," she answered, her voice shaking. She tried to return to the car, but Chris planted his hands on her shoulders and stopped her. "Let me go."

"No," he whispered firmly. "You've jumped to a lot of conclusions tonight, and I'll be damned if I understand why. But just for the record, sweetheart, *nothing* is going back to the way it was. That little girl over there is mine, too. And if I have to hire a lawyer and have blood tests and fight you for a share of her custody, that's what I'll do."

Frozen fingers clutched her heart and squeezed. "No judge in his right mind will give custody rights to a wandering actor who never stays in one place long enough to buy furniture," she managed to whisper furiously.

"No?" His smile didn't reach his eyes. "Do you want to risk it in court?"

Anne swallowed hard as a cold chill shook her. "You wouldn't do that."

"You decided twelve years ago that I wasn't good father material." Pain flashed across the shadows of his face. "You deliberately left me out of your life, and Martha's, too. Don't you think that hurts?" When she didn't answer, he continued. "You're not making the decisions by yourself anymore. For some reason you think I'm taking Martha away from you, I'll be damned if I know why. Or even how you think such a thing is possible."

"You want to take her on the tour."

"She has a lot of talent. How can you deny that?"

"I don't. I just want her to be a normal child."

He dropped his hands, releasing her. "Being able to sing doesn't make her a freak. Why don't you let Martha decide what kind of child she wants to be? What are you so afraid of?"

She shook her head. "I'm not packing up for a seventy-city tour, and neither is Martha. We're at the same place we were twelve years ago. We want different things out of life. I guess we always did."

"You're telling me that what we had this summer is over?"

"There were never any promises." He'd never talked of the future, and neither had she. She'd been deluding herself, thinking she could love him and not get hurt.

Chris shuddered and took a deep breath. When he finally spoke his voice was low. "I have loved you for years. I guess it's time I got over it."

Anne couldn't answer. She swirled around and hurried to the car, hoping the darkness would hide the tears from her daughter. Praying the inky night would hide the pain in her eyes.

"MOM, YOU DON'T look very good." Martha handed her the bundle of envelopes she'd retrieved from the mailbox. "Can you and Chris make up?"

Anne took the letters and tossed them on the kitchen table. "We're not teenagers, Marty. We've had a difference in opinion and have decided not to see each other anymore." Which was breaking her heart, she added silently. Saying goodbye to him twice in one lifetime hurt more than she'd ever thought possible.

Martha pointed to the table. "Aren't you going to read the mail?"

"Not now." Anne looked out the window toward the garden. She hadn't weeded or watered in three days. Besides, the sun hurt her eyes.

"I think you should."

Anne turned back to Martha and realized guiltily that the child appeared very worried. "I'm sorry, honey. I guess I haven't been very good company for the past few days." She gave Martha a big smile. "Maybe we could go out for ice cream. Would you like to do that?"

"I think you'd better read the mail," Martha insisted.

"All right." She walked over to the table and thumbed through the envelopes. An electric bill, two advertisements and a long white envelope with the theater's return address in the corner. Anne picked it up, seeing her name scrawled across the front in unfamiliar writing. No stamp, meaning someone had put the envelope in her mailbox. She slid open the flap and pulled out three maroon-and-white tickets.

"Are those tickets to the show?"

"Yes," Anne said, reading the date. Thursday. "They're for tonight." She looked in the envelope for a note, but there was nothing else. "Chris must have sent them."

Martha's face lit up. "We can go, can't we? I mean, he sent three tickets. One for you, one for me and one for Grandpa. He promised me I could see the show. And I even met the man who's going to be inside the big plant."

Anne shook her head and replaced the tickets in the envelope. She didn't think she was ready to face him again. Not yet, not while the pain was still so close to the surface. "I don't think it's a very good idea."

"You're not being *fair!*" Martha glared at her and stomped out of the kitchen, slamming the back door shut after her. Anne watched out the window as Martha ran across the yard toward Nancy and Lisa's house.

Dan poked his head in from the living room. "What was that all about?"

"Martha doesn't think I'm being fair." She sighed, picking up the envelope again. "Chris sent tickets to the show tonight."

Dan's eyebrows rose. "He did? I thought you two had a fight." He came closer and put his arms around her. "I know you haven't wanted to talk about it, but I'm here if you need me." He backed up and eyed her. "And you sure look like you need a friend."

"He wants the legal right to see her."

"I guess he simply wants to be part of your lives."

"But what if he takes her away from me?"

"Chris loves you, and he loves Martha. He wouldn't knowingly hurt either one of you." Dan tightened his hands on her shoulders, steadying her. "And you love him—don't deny it. How can all that love be wrong?"

"I promised Chris I'd tell Martha that he's her father, but I just couldn't do it."

"You should keep your promises. After all this time, you know you need to be fair. Listen to me," he insisted. "Life's short. Take it from an expert, Annie-girl."

"I don't think it's that simple," she began, when the ringing of the phone interrupted her. "Hello," she said, then listened intently. When she hung up she turned to her father. "That was the principal of the high school. I got a job teaching English."

"Congratulations!" he cried, his face lighting with happiness. "I know how badly you wanted it."

"Yes," Anne agreed, leaning against the counter. She had exactly what she wanted: a home, a garden and a full-time teaching job. Security, accomplished at last. So why did she feel like crying?

And how would she tell Martha the truth?

"I TOLD Marie I'd be there," Dan said, taking one of the tickets from the envelope and tucking it inside his sport jacket.

"You look very nice."

"Don't wait up. I may sing at cabaret tonight, if they need me."

Anne chuckled. "I have the feeling they wouldn't dare turn you down."

"Age has its merits," he said, heading toward the front door. "Good luck."

"Thanks." She'd decided to talk to Martha tonight. She owed the child and Chris that much. Somehow she'd have to believe that he wouldn't do anything to hurt his daughter, that he wanted what was best for her, even if he didn't agree with Anne's idea of what was best.

She hated lying to her daughter, and could no longer rationalize hiding the truth. It was time all of them knew where they stood. Chris, Martha and her father were right: she was not being fair. It was time she realized that and did something about it.

"Martha!" She went down the hall and heard the bathtub water running.

"What? I'm taking a bubble bath!"

"Never mind," Anne said. "We'll talk when you're done."

The child's voice sounded muffled. "I might be a long time. I'm really dirty."

"That's okay." Anne didn't mind the reprieve. She'd have more time to figure out how she would begin the conversation. Her stomach tensed at what was ahead. "Take your time."

Half an hour later Anne could wait no longer. She knocked on the bathroom door again. "Martha, I want you to come out now. I, uh, need to talk to you."

Silence was the only response. Annoyed, Anne twisted the doorknob. She'd had enough of her daughter's silent treatment. "If you don't answer, I'm coming in." Nothing. Alarmed, Anne pushed open the door.

The room was empty. The only sign that Martha had been there was the pile of dirty clothes on the floor.

Anne hurried back to the kitchen and found the envelope on the counter. Only one ticket remained inside, so Anne knew exactly where her headstrong daughter had gone. She hurried to her room to change. If she was going to haul Martha out of the theater, she'd better not do it in her nightgown.

THE DOUBLE DOORS were closed by the time she arrived at the theater, so she opened one quietly and tiptoed into the lobby. Marie peeked around the corner, a smile lighting her face when she saw her.

"I'm so glad you're feeling better," she whispered. "You've missed almost half the show, though. Why don't you just slip into a seat in the balcony until after intermission?"

"Is Martha here?"

"She's with Chris, in the back."

"Thank goodness. I don't know what I would have done if she wasn't here."

"You didn't know?"

"She sneaked out."

"Oh, dear." Marie shook her head. "Dan was a little surprised to see her here, but he thought you'd changed your mind and dropped her off to see the show."

"No. Martha's in big trouble."

Applause sounded from the other side of the wall. "Intermission," Marie informed her. "They should be coming out in a minute."

Anne moved to the wall with the cast photographs on it. "I'll wait right here."

The lobby soon filled with people on their way outside to the cool ocean-scented air, but Anne spotted

Chris easily. His white shirt was rolled up at the sleeves and his dark tie loosened slightly at the neck. He appeared uncomfortably warm, but his mouth curved into a smile as he guided Martha through the crowd. Anne moved toward them, crossing their path to the porch.

"Goody," Martha chirped, grinning at her mother.

"You're in a lot of trouble, young lady," Anne told her. "I don't know why you're smiling."

Chris stared at Anne, then down at Martha. "What's going on?"

"She sneaked out of the house to come here tonight."

"Martha?" He tilted her chin with one finger so she had to look at him.

"I did it on purpose," she declared, grinning up at him. "To get you two together again."

He dropped his hand and cupped her shoulder. "Maybe we'd better talk about this somewhere a little more private. Come on." They followed him outside, down the steps and to the back of the stage, around the corner to the familiar sheltered area of the lilac bush.

"You are grounded until school starts," Anne muttered. "And maybe even after that, until the end of the year."

"I just wanted you to make up," Martha wailed, her eyes filling with tears. "You're my parents, and I wanted you to be together like you were this summer."

"You told her?" they asked each other in unison.

"Of course not," Chris replied.

"I was going to do that tonight," Anne said. "I was waiting for her to finish her bath."

"Then how . . ."

Martha glared at both of them. "I figured it out a couple of weeks ago. Do you think I'm dumb or something? Grandpa's scrapbook has pictures of him at this theater twelve years ago." She looked at her mother. "I figured you must have been with him and Grandma then. And I *know* when I was born." She glanced at Chris. "It takes nine months to have a baby. We learned that in science. And you *said* you knew each other a long time ago. Why didn't you tell me?"

"I didn't know how," Anne admitted. "I wanted to make sure you'd understand, but I didn't have the words." She looked at Chris for help. "I guess I still don't."

Chris didn't seem to have that problem. "Your mother and I loved each other very much that summer. It was the best summer of my life, except for this one." He grinned and Martha grinned back. "I was offered a job on a European tour and I asked your mother to go with me, but she wanted to go back to college and be a teacher. So, even though we loved each other, we said goodbye. Only we didn't know we were going to have a baby. Your mother decided not to tell me because I was so far away."

"But you found out," Martha said.

"Yes. Your mother told me this summer, but we decided not to tell you until after *Music Man* was over."

"That was dumb."

Anne couldn't help smiling. "Maybe, a little. But I was trying to do what was best for you."

Chris Bogart's daughter made a face. "You *knew* I liked him."

"Yes. I should have known it would be all right."

Chris opened his arms. "Come here, kid." She flew into his embrace, her long hair tangling against his arms. After a long minute he released her, took her by the shoulders and pointed her toward the theater. "Go find your grandfather and watch the show with him. I need to talk to your mother." When she opened her mouth to protest, he stopped her. "I want to talk to your mother *alone*."

"Okay, Daddy!" She giggled at the shocked expression on his face and ran off toward the cobblestone path.

"Daddy," he echoed.

"You have what you wanted," Anne said. Suddenly she was very, very tired.

"Not exactly." He held out his hand. "Come here. You're too far away."

She took his hand and let him draw her closer so she stood directly in front of him, close enough to feel the heat from his skin.

"I don't want to let you go," he murmured, his dark gaze on her face. "I made that mistake last time. I don't want to lose you again."

"I'm not the one leaving," she said.

He tried to smile. "Neither am I. Dennis is taking the tour. Aside from a few trips to New York, I'm staying here to organize next year's season and a thousand other things. Like giving a certain little girl dance lessons."

"Martha will love that."

"What about Martha's mother?"

"She has to let her daughter start making some of her own decisions."

"Like trying out for the road production of *Music Man?*"

Anne winced. "Not necessarily."

"Good," he said. "She told me she didn't want to hurt my feelings, but she wanted to stay home and try out for soccer instead. Seems the girls next door have filled her in on the local sports schedule."

She couldn't hide her relief. "It's good for her to have friends."

"Now, about us. I've done a lot of thinking, Annie." He cupped her face, smoothing the dark gold hair away from her cheek. "I can't predict the future, but I can promise to love you forever. With my entire being. I can't promise to be home for dinner at five every night, but if we love each other we could work out whatever problems we'll have."

"I accepted a teaching job today. Is that a problem?"

"Not to me," he assured her. "You'll have summers off while I'm working here." His voice softened. "Do you love me, Annie?"

The easiest question to answer. "Oh, yes," she replied, before his lips touched hers.

"Wait," he said, hesitating. "You've got to understand, this is a permanent role. As Mrs. Bogart."

Anne reached up and pulled him close. "Do you think I can handle the part?"

"I think you're perfect for it."

HARLEQUIN®

Temptation®
IS TEN!

Join the festivities as Harlequin celebrates
Temptation's tenth anniversary in 1994!

Look for tempting treats from your favorite
Temptation authors all year long. The celebration
begins with Passion's Quest—four exciting sensual
stories featuring the most elemental passions....

The temptation continues with Lost Loves, a sizzling
miniseries about love lost...love found. And watch for
the 500th Temptation in July by bestselling author
Rita Clay Estrada, a seductive story in the vein
of the much-loved tale, THE IVORY KEY.

In May, look for details of an irresistible offer:
three classic Temptation novels by Rita Clay Estrada,
Glenda Sanders and Gina Wilkins in a collector's
hardcover edition—free with proof of purchase!

After ten tempting years, *nobody* can resist

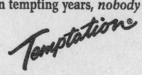

Where do you find hot Texas nights, smooth Texas charm and dangerously sexy cowboys?

Crystal Creek reverberates with the exciting rhythm of Texas. Each story features the rugged individuals who live and love in the Lone Star state.

"...Crystal Creek wonderfully evokes the hot days and steamy nights of a small Texas community...impossible to put down until the last page is turned."
                                                                    —*Romantic Times*

"...a series that should hook any romance reader. Outstanding."
                                                                    —*Rendezvous*

"Altogether, it couldn't be better."   —*Rendezvous*

Don't miss the next book in this exciting series.
SHAMELESS by SANDY STEEN

Available in July wherever Harlequin books are sold.

HARLEQUIN®
Temptation

Lost Loves

RIGHT MAN...WRONG TIME

Remember that one man who turned your world upside down. Who made you experience all the ecstatic highs of passion and lows of loss and regret. What if you met him again?

You dared to lose your heart once and had it broken. Dare you love again?

JoAnn Ross, Glenda Sanders, Rita Clay Estrada, Gina Wilkins and Carin Rafferty. Find their stories in Lost Loves, Temptation's newest miniseries, running May to September 1994.

In July, experience *Forms of Love* by Rita Clay Estrada, Book #500 from Temptation! Dan Lovejoy had lost his wife in a tragic accident—then he met her double. Only this woman who looked like Kendra wasn't Kendra. Moreover, she had some very *unusual* secrets of her own. Dan couldn't help himself—he started to fall in love with her. But who was he falling in love with? A moving, romantic story in the tradition of *The Ivory Key*.

What if...?

LOST3

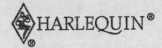

EXPECTATIONS
Shannon Waverly

Eternity, Massachusetts, is a town with something special going for it. According to legend, those who marry in Eternity's chapel are destined for a lifetime of happiness. As long as the legend holds true, couples will continue to flock here to marry and local businesses will thrive.

Unfortunately for the town, Marion and Geoffrey Kent are about to prove the legend wrong!

EXPECTATIONS, available in July from Harlequin Romance®, is the second book in Harlequin's new cross-line series, **WEDDINGS, INC.** Be sure to look for the third book, **WEDDING SONG,** by Vicki Lewis Thompson (Harlequin Temptation® #502), coming in August.

New York Times Bestselling Author

BARBARA DELINSKY

**Look for her at your favorite retail outlet this
September with**

A SINGLE ROSE

A two-week Caribbean treasure hunt with rugged and
sexy Noah VanBaar wasn't Shaye Burke's usual style.
Stuck with Noah on a beat-up old sloop with no engine,
she was left feeling both challenged and confused. Torn
between passion and self-control, Shaye was afraid of
being swept away by an all-consuming love.

Available in September, wherever Harlequin books are sold.

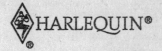

HARLEQUIN®

Don't miss these Harlequin favorites by some of our most
distinguished authors!
And now, you can receive a discount by ordering two or more titles!

HT #25551	THE OTHER WOMAN by Candace Schuler	$2.99	☐
HT #25539	FOOLS RUSH IN by Vicki Lewis Thompson	$2.99	☐
HP #11550	THE GOLDEN GREEK by Sally Wentworth	$2.89	☐
HP #11603	PAST ALL REASON by Kay Thorpe	$2.99	☐
HR #03228	MEANT FOR EACH OTHER by Rebecca Winters	$2.89	☐
HR #03268	THE BAD PENNY by Susan Fox	$2.99	☐
HS #70532	TOUCH THE DAWN by Karen Young	$3.39	☐
HS #70540	FOR THE LOVE OF IVY by Barbara Kaye	$3.39	☐
HI #22177	MINDGAME by Laura Pender	$2.79	☐
HI #22214	TO DIE FOR by M.J. Rodgers	$2.89	☐
HAR #16421	HAPPY NEW YEAR, DARLING by Margaret St. George	$3.29	☐
HAR #16507	THE UNEXPECTED GROOM by Muriel Jensen	$3.50	☐
HH #28774	SPINDRIFT by Miranda Jarrett	$3.99	☐
HH #28782	SWEET SENSATIONS by Julie Tetel	$3.99	☐

Harlequin Promotional Titles

#83259	UNTAMED MAVERICK HEARTS	$4.99	☐

(Short-story collection featuring Heather Graham Pozzessere,
Patricia Potter, Joan Johnston)
(limited quantities available on certain titles)

	AMOUNT	$
DEDUCT:	10% DISCOUNT FOR 2+ BOOKS	$
	POSTAGE & HANDLING	$
	($1.00 for one book, 50¢ for each additional)	
	APPLICABLE TAXES*	$ _____
	TOTAL PAYABLE	$ _____

(check or money order—please do not send cash)

To order, complete this form and send it, along with a check or money order for the
total above, payable to Harlequin Books, to: **in the U.S.:** 3010 Walden Avenue,
P.O. Box 9047, Buffalo, NY 14269-9047; **in Canada:** P.O. Box 613, Fort Erie, Ontario,
L2A 5X3.

Name: _____

Address: _____ City: _____

State/Prov.: _____ Zip/Postal Code: _____

*New York residents remit applicable sales taxes.
Canadian residents remit applicable GST and provincial taxes.

HBACK-AJ

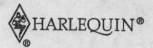

Fifty red-blooded, white-hot, true-blue hunks
from every State in the Union!

Look for MEN MADE IN AMERICA! Written by some of
our most popular authors, these stories feature fifty of
the strongest, sexiest men, each from a different state in
the union!

Two titles available every other month at your favorite
retail outlet.

In May, look for:

KISS YESTERDAY GOODBYE by Leigh Michaels (Iowa)
A TIME TO KEEP by Curtiss Ann Matlock (Kansas)

In June, look for:

ONE PALE, FAWN GLOVE by Linda Shaw (Kentucky)
BAYOU MIDNIGHT by Emilie Richards (Louisiana)

You won't be able to resist MEN MADE IN AMERICA!